"I'm all yours," Eric said, smiling

"You bet you are," Danni muttered under her breath. How'd he do it? How was he able to look so sincere, almost loving? She shook her head and forced a smile. "I have the rope in my bag."

His gaze left her breasts and he met her eyes. He leaned back on the pillows and stretched naked before her. "You came prepared."

He didn't know the half of it.

He smelled of arousal. Danni knew he wouldn't get away, but that didn't make what she was about to do any less daunting. She tied his arms and legs to the bedposts. But desire was almost killing her. She couldn't stall any longer. "You picked the wrong mark, ace."

"Mark? What are you talking about?"

"You seduced me to get to my father, Eric. And now you're going to pay."

Blaze™

Dear Reader,

A favorite game I like to play is two truths and a lie. For some reason, the lie part is always more fun to tell. Danni Flynn is a woman who likes telling lies, too. Actually, playing a con comes as easily to her as eating chocolate. Yet she craves normalcy, in life and in relationships. Mysterious and sexy Eric Reynolds seems to fill the bill nicely. But does this "good boy" seem a little too excited by her naughty side?

As for my favorite game, see if you can spot which statement is the lie. It felt great to write *Hitting the Mark* and draw upon knowledge gained from my somewhat checkered past for something useful. It can be difficult to sound casual and not panicked when explaining my knowledge of what the back of a police car looks like (both marked and unmarked). It's simply a coincidence. And third, it's thrilling to see another Blaze of mine in print. Or are they all true?

I love to hear from readers. Please e-mail jill@jillmonroebooks.com or visit me at www.jillmonroebooks.com or on my blog at jillmonroe.blogspot.com.

Jill

HITTING THE MARK

Jill Monroe

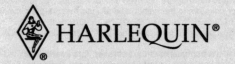

HARLEQUIN®

TORONTO • NEW YORK • LONDON
AMSTERDAM • PARIS • SYDNEY • HAMBURG
STOCKHOLM • ATHENS • TOKYO • MILAN • MADRID
PRAGUE • WARSAW • BUDAPEST • AUCKLAND

ISBN-13: 978-0-373-79308-2
ISBN-10:   0-373-79308-1

HITTING THE MARK

This edition published by arrangement with Harlequin Books S.A.

® and TM are trademarks of the publisher. Trademarks indicated with
® are registered in the United States Patent and Trademark Office, the
Canadian Trade Marks Office and in other countries.

www.eHarlequin.com

Printed in U.S.A.

ABOUT THE AUTHOR

Jill Monroe makes her home in Oklahoma with her family. When not writing, she spends way too much time on the Internet completing "research" or updating her blog. Even when writing, she's thinking of ways to avoid cooking.

Books by Jill Monroe

HARLEQUIN BLAZE
245—SHARE THE DARKNESS

HARLEQUIN TEMPTATION
1003—NEVER NAUGHTY ENOUGH

Don't miss any of our special offers. Write to us at the following address for information on our newest releases.

Harlequin Reader Service
U.S.: 3010 Walden Ave., P.O. Box 1325, Buffalo, NY 14269
Canadian: P.O. Box 609, Fort Erie, Ont. L2A 5X3

This book is dedicated to my husband.
Thanks for always believing in me!

A special thanks to Gena Showalter.
The sun and moon don't lie. Thanks also go to
Kassia Krozser, who knows all my dirt and
therefore gets in every dedication.
Plus you're an awesome friend.

I'd also like to thank Sheila Fields, Linda Rooks,
Betty, Donnell, Tami and Amanda. To OKP,
whenever I imagined all the bad things
happening to Dirk, I pictured your face.

Many thanks to Kathryn Lye. I'm looking
forward to the next one!

To my family, who are so patient and supportive—
I love you.

Prologue

MAYBE SHE SHOULD just fake it.

Danni Flynn closed her eyes and willed herself to get into the mood. She concentrated on the sensual play of the hard muscles of her lover's back as he moved his tongue along her body. She loved running her fingers over his hips. Loved to feel him push against her when she found his ultra-sensitive spots.

Except this time, all she felt was betrayed.

Danni tried to shut off her mind, made herself slow down to enjoy the delicious heat of his breath on her neck as he whispered, "Danni, you're so incredible."

When his fingers found her nipple and gently caressed, her toes curled, actually curled into the mattress.

Okay, maybe she wouldn't have to fake it. Maybe she could let this go on a little longer. She *could* get back into it. After all, Eric Reynolds, if that were really his name, owed her the mother of all orgasms considering what he'd done to her.

Thinking of his treachery caused her muscles to tense.

"Something wrong?" he asked. He looked so good.

All messed up from their lovemaking and concerned about her. *Jerk.*

"Everything's…wonderful," she lied.

But she'd lost it again. There had to be some way to keep her brain from drifting to the lying, manipulating and using jerk Eric was. Rather than the orgasm-inducing God of Sex that he'd proven to be in the past.

He continued to caress and behave in ways that never failed to get a response from her. Never failed until now. From the determination on his face, Eric wasn't going to stop until she came. That was what made him a great lover. Made being the operative word there. Past tense. This was the last time she'd allow him to touch her.

"You feel so good, Danni," he said, his voice nothing but a sexy ragged whisper.

Yeah, she just bet she did. A wave of anger killed the last of her pleasure buzz. Would it feel good when she duct taped his mouth?

Yep, fake it. She sighed and made a moan deep in her throat to speed things along.

He now moved inside her more purposefully, his breathing becoming more strained. She almost grinned. He'd bought it. This faking business wasn't going to be so difficult. Who'd ever invented it sure had the right idea. Add a moan here and there and he'd be done.

Now wait a minute. Why should the lying bastard be having any fun? If she didn't get to come, he shouldn't, either. In fact, she'd never planned to let him enjoy this one last marathon of sex. Honestly, as long

as he was screwing her *outside* of bed, she should at least get one last good screw from him in bed.

And now *that* wasn't even working. Might as well jump to phase two of her plan.

Determined, she gripped his strong shoulders. Danni pushed him away, their bodies still joined.

"I have a game I want to play," she said, dropping her voice to a provocative level.

A wicked glint sparked to life in his brown eyes. "You and your games."

"I want to tie you up and then do naughty things to your body," she told him as she traced a teasing line across his chest.

"Next time," he said, his voice a promise.

She shook her head, turning her smile devilish. "No, it will be more fun this way. Our bodies will ache for completion, but we won't let them have it until we turn up the heat even more. It will be almost tantric."

Eric groaned deep in his throat. "I can never say no to you."

Yeah, it was dealing with the truth he had a problem with. Double dealing with the truth.

Eric wrapped his arms around her, and for a moment she closed her eyes. Remembering. Remembering what it felt like to wake up in his arms this very morning thinking he loved her. Knowing she loved him. The solid strength of him. The promise of a future in his eyes. That sexy, sleepy smile on his face only for her.

He rolled so she straddled him. She gasped in pleasure as he delved deeper into her. Okay, the man

had skills in bed. Her last boyfriend had never mastered the roll-over-and-still-stay-joined maneuver. Although that boyfriend had been upfront about his loserness and lack of ambition.

"I'm all yours," he said.

"You just bet you will be."

"What?" he asked, his eyes dark and lusty.

How'd he do it? Just how in the hell was he able to look so sincere, almost loving while all the time he was also happy to send her on a train ride to hell?

Danni shook her head and forced a smile. "Nothing. I have the rope in my bag," she told him.

His gaze left her breasts and he met her eyes. His brows lifted. "You came prepared."

He didn't know the half of it.

He groaned again as she shimmied off his body. She fought back the wave of sadness, already missing the intimate closeness of being joined. She'd use an extra piece of duct tape on his mouth just for that feeling alone.

His gaze followed her as she padded along the carpet to her bag. Originally, she was going to tie him up after he'd given her a great time. Gripping the handle of the bag hard in frustration, she tossed it on the bedside table. Returning to the bed, she schooled her features to look seductive. Her eyes promised the naughty game-playing he liked so much. With a snap, Danni pulled out the rope. Thick, tight and knotted.

He blinked in surprise. "You're serious. I expected a scarf or something," he said, excitement lacing his words.

She'd like to hog-tie him. That is, if she actually knew how to do such a thing. Hog-tie him and beat him with a stick like he had her heart.

She sucked in the side of her lip. Now that was being a bit overdramatic. Even for her.

She winked then reached over and drew out a few delicate scarves. "The scarf I'll put against your skin." *Jerk.* "That way you won't get chafed." *Rot in hell.* "Wouldn't want you showing up to work with burn marks." *And may it fall off.*

Oh, no, she couldn't let him show up for work looking less than corporate. Especially since she knew now just how important that job of his was to him. He could lie and cheat and then sleep like a baby. That's a skill even *she* didn't possess.

A hint of uncertainty lit in his eyes. "Trust me," she urged, throwing back the same words he used on her half a dozen times.

Eric lifted his hand, and she forced her expression to stay sensual rather than triumphant. *Yes. It was working.*

Danni pressed a quick kiss on the warm skin of his wrist then slid the scarf in place. He even had sexy wrists, masculine and flexible with the right amount of hair. Oh, it was so unfair. With a quick twist, she secured his arm to the bedpost and used the same routine to bind his other arm and both his legs. Sitting back on her heels on Eric's large bed, she admired her work.

Despite being such a jerk, Eric Reynolds was the best looking man she'd ever seen. Sprawled against the king-sized bed, his arms and legs tied up, he exuded

power and force. Only a man utterly confident in his own strength and had trust in his woman would allow himself to be tied up. That's what she'd counted on.

There'd be hell to pay if she didn't work this one right.

Locks of his dark hair fell across his forehead, and she allowed herself one more time to touch the strands, stroke the hair away from his face. She trailed one finger along his sexy cheekbone and the harsh outline of his jaw. His lips, he had such beautiful lips. Wicked lips that made her want to do erotic things. Wicked lips because they told such wicked lies.

Eric sucked in a breath as she leisurely traced a path along his broad chest, and the flatness of his stomach. She smiled as she saw his penis rise, then harden even more. The only place he didn't lie. But that was because he couldn't. She tore her gaze from his body, focused once more on his lips.

One last kiss. She needed one more kiss to remind her what betrayal tasted like. Danni bent over and slid her tongue on his bottom lip. Despite being restrained, he moved his mouth so he kissed her fully. Her heartbeat quickened, and she felt her nipples tingle and tighten. He made her feel things. Want things.

And that's why she had to do this. Why she couldn't congratulate him on his great con and walk away. Because for a few short days he made her dreams come true, but then snatched them away.

The sounds of their ragged breathing filled his bedroom. She quickly broke contact and scrambled off him.

Frantic, Danni searched for her panties. Damn, that was one part of her plan she hadn't fully thought through. But then, neither had she made allowances for ditching her clothes in such a hurry, and leaving them all over his suite.

"What are you doing?" Eric asked, his voice curious and oh, so trusting.

Forget her panties. Grabbing her jeans, she swiftly stepped into them and zipped them up. She didn't look at him. "What do you think I'm doing? I'm getting dressed."

"What?" Eric managed to sit up higher, his expression growing serious. She'd given too much slack in the legs. Oh, well. Hindsight.

After donning her bra and hastily buttoning her shirt, Danni slipped into her shoes. "I'm leaving."

"What the hell…? Danni, this isn't funny." Eric tugged furiously at his bonds. They held. *Good.*

She finally met his gaze. "I'm not meaning it to be a joke," she told him, her voice steady and sure.

Eric struggled against the rope. He must have realized she wasn't playing.

"I wasn't lying about being a Scout," she said. "I really do know how to make good knots. Don't worry, despite the Do Not Disturb sign I placed on the knob, I'll call room service to come get you. After a few hours. That should give you plenty of time to reflect on your crimes."

Cold, controlled anger replaced confusion in his eyes. A wave of unease made her shiver. She had to get

out of there. *Now.* But she couldn't have him yelling the place down. It was time to tape his mouth shut. Reaching for the roll, she made her way back to the bed. With every step she took, tension filled her.

"What are you planning to do with that?" he asked. He smelled of arousal, and now, unforgiving male. She knew he couldn't get away, but that didn't make the man's intimidating presence any less daunting.

She unrolled a long strip of duct tape.

"Danni, stop this. You're making a mistake," he blurted.

Danni shook her head. "I doubt it. You picked the wrong mark, ace."

"Mark? What are you talking about?"

"Someone has to save my father."

"Danni, whatever it is you think you know, you're wrong. Let me expl—"

"Save your explanation. It will all just be more lies."

His eyes widened in surprise, and she grabbed at the opportunity to secure his mouth.

"What is it you once told me, Eric? You didn't believe in chance. Well, you made a convert. I don't believe in chance either. Only making my own opportunities. And I'm making one now. You seduced me to get to my father, and now you're going to pay."

1

Two Weeks Earlier

DANNI BALANCED the laundry basket on her hip as she stepped out of the dry Nevada heat, and into the humidity of the Save 'n' Wash. No one did their laundry on a Wednesday afternoon, so it was the perfect time to study. For some reason, just starting school when most people her age would have been finishing made her feel a twinge unsure. Funny how going straight could do that to a person. She'd always felt cool and in control while on the grift.

She'd been born to play the game. Or so her father had always told her. And taught her.

Not worth thinking about now. Danni blinked to allow her eyes to adjust to the inside light, and set her basket down on an empty table. Her textbook lay on top of her dirty clothes. She had more than two years ahead of her, but she wouldn't have it any other way.

She'd carefully pushed her change into the slot, when a shadow fell across her arm.

"Do you have any dryer sheets? I must have left mine back at the hotel."

Danni glanced up to match the sexy voice to the shadow. She had heard some pickup lines before, in fact, she'd heard that exact pickup line in the Laundromat, but never from someone like this. Someone who didn't need cheesy words because his very presence was an open invitation.

Tall and dark and rugged.

Her breath hitched. She'd always gone for the rebels. Long hair, no job and an air of total irresponsibility. Bonus points for lack of sensitivity, except for something useless like his bad music or his dirty poetry. Those were the kind of guys who rocked her world.

But this wasn't a guy. This was a man.

Despite the corporate cut to his dark hair, he exuded a jagged undercurrent of danger. No rebellion…just promise. She swallowed. This man was gulp worthy. A snug, navy T-shirt molded his proud chest and shoulders. Danni kept a tight rein on her eyes. *Do not lower.*

She met his gaze. She found humor in the darkness of his brown eyes. And expectation. Oh yeah, he was waiting on her to answer. Dryer sheet. That was it.

Time to work it.

"For a dollar," she told him.

He raised an eyebrow. "You want a dollar for one dryer sheet?"

Danni shrugged. "You're welcome to go to the store."

A touch of frustration mixed with the humor already in his eyes. He stuffed his fingers into the front pocket of his well-worn jeans. And they fit him well. Nice flat

stomach, narrow hips. Fine-looking package. Okay, so she looked lower. Big deal. He pulled out a five.

"I can even make you change," she said with a smile.

She could imagine it right now. Slide him three bucks and a dryer sheet, pocket the extra. Daddy had taught her well.

But she wouldn't. Because damn it, she was determined to be an honest person.

Also, a very rude one. Rudeness kept people away, and that's how she liked it. It was the way it had to be. When people got close to you, they began expecting things. Wanting to know personal, private details.

He pushed the money into her hand. His long, lean fingers warm and strong as he folded her fingers around the cash. "If you need it that badly, keep the whole five." The man took one of her sheets, turned his back and tossed it into one of the oversized dryers in the corner.

He looked just as good from the back as he did from the front.

Shoving the bill into her pocket, Danni was at a loss. She'd come out on top in this little encounter. Hadn't she?

Danni grabbed her book and sat. Freeing her mind to the wide-open world of court reporting, she tried to forget the man. She should be memorizing the abbreviation for parenthesis. She had a mock deposition to study for. Uh-huh, that was irony there.

Her gaze strayed to the man folding his socks. What if he started folding his underwear? What if he didn't?

Despite the thinness of her T-shirt, she broke out in a light sweat. This was a man who deserved underwear speculation. He also took the fun out of it by giving her all five bucks.

And yet that made him even sexier.

Maybe she hadn't needed to be *that* rude. But the man stirred up every instinct not to talk to him. Perhaps that was a good thing—her track record with men was awful. And she always went with her gut. So should she go against it for once, and go for him instead? The last of his clothes were already dry, there wouldn't be much more of an opportunity.

Grabbing a dryer sheet, she walked to the table where he stood shaking out another pair of well-worn jeans. He didn't react as she approached. She waved the dryer sheet in his field of vision. The flowery scent of a summer day wafted between them. At least that was the scent mentioned on the package.

Mr. Gorgeous turned toward her and raised an eyebrow.

"I'm waving the dryer sheet white flag of peace. Maybe I was a little rude back there."

"A little?" he asked, his voice low and rumbly. And very, very sexy.

"It should be two dryer sheets for a dollar. I mis-quoted the price earlier." Okay, if he could work "dryer sheets" into a cheesy pickup line, so could she.

Without touching her, he tugged the sheet from her fingers.

In spite of the white flag, she refused to give up.

"Actually, the going rate for five dollars is two dryer sheets and a cup of coffee." She reached into her pocket and pulled out his bill. "And I just happen to have five dollars."

"I just happen to be thirsty." The humor reappeared in his dark eyes.

"There's a coffee shop at the end of this block. Why don't I meet you there in about thirty minutes? My clothes should be dry by then."

"Thirty minutes it is," he told her.

But she knew the truth. *He wouldn't show up.* Sure, he'd accepted, but then who wouldn't in order to get the crazy person at the Laundromat away from them? Besides, he was definitely corporate. Corporate never went for her.

TWENTY-FIVE MINUTES LATER, Danni slid her laundry basket with clean clothes into the trunk of her car and slammed the lid. She turned and faced the street. Five minutes to go. She couldn't seem too eager. She dug out her cell phone and dialed Cassie's number.

"I've asked someone out for coffee," Danni said as soon as her best friend answered.

"It's snowing outside, right?"

Danni checked the sunny blue sky. "What are you talking about? It's way past snowing in Reno."

"That was sort of my point. You never get my jokes. How did this come about?"

"I insulted him, took his money, then apologized without really apologizing."

"That's like my last three relationships," Cassie said, her teasing voice making Danni grin.

"He won't show," Danni said.

"Whew, that's better. For a minute there I was afraid you were nervous. But then, your normal cynicism reappeared."

"Nerves give men the upper hand on a date." Was this a date? Meeting? Whatever. Nerves were never good. "You can never show them that you like them."

"Absolutely. Dating suicide."

"Do I detect a bit of facetiousness in your voice?"

"If you only detect a bit, then you need your hearing tested. Listen, Danni, since you've asked this guy out and that's a first for you, why don't you make this a date of firsts. Here's a guy who knows nothing of your past. He's not going to be judging you. You're just a woman, he's just a man. Enjoy each other's company. Enjoy the moment. Why are you talking to me when there's a man waiting for you? I'm hanging up now." *Click.*

She smiled as she closed her cell. Cassie was probably right. Danni hadn't consciously decided to treat this new guy differently than every other man who'd stumbled into her life. But she had, and that was a valid reason to be nervous.

After putting her phone back into her purse, Danni locked her car and headed to the coffee shop, leisurely passing by others on the sidewalk. Actually, the coffee shop was more like a bistro, with a selection of breads, teas and coffees. An electronic chime sounded as she strolled through the door.

Normally her glance would head straight for the refrigerated display cabinet, then she'd stop and look at the specials written on the chalkboard, or take a sample of the bread of the week. Not today. Instead, her gaze went directly to the seating area filled with fashionable glass-topped wrought-iron tables and matching chairs.

He *was* there.

He'd waited for her. Her steps slowed for a moment as she approached him lounging against one of the high-backed barstools. Her knees turned wobbly all of a sudden and she hadn't expected that.

So, how should she play this? Classic vamp? No, that wouldn't work—she wasn't wearing the right shoes. Girl next door? No, she'd already blown her chance at innocence back at the Laundromat. She paused and that's when he looked directly at her. He smiled. A slow, open smile that moved across those sexy, sensuous lips of his and every nerve ending in her body fired up.

She'd been right to be cynical. She'd been right to push him away at the beginning because this man was dangerous. This was the kind of man who made logical women say, "Sure, I'll invest everything I own in your pyramid scheme."

She had no clue how to angle her behavior. Cassie had suggested that Danni should just be a woman. Could it ever be that simple? Just be yourself. Whoever that was.

Danni realized she was smiling back. *I'm an idiot.* She slid into the stool beside him, and the waitress came by and asked for their order.

"You took my money and I don't even know your name," he said after a moment of silence.

"Danielle, but everyone calls me Danni."

"I'm Eric."

She shook his hand, his fingers feeling softly calloused. "So, Eric, do you usually pick up women while doing your laundry?"

A moment passed before he answered, his body relaxed. "Only on Wednesdays. Thursdays it's the grocery store. Besides, that wasn't a pickup."

"It wasn't?" Her feet began to tap under the table. Had he spotted something in her the way she had in him?

"You were the only person in the place using dryer sheets. Everyone else had the liquid stuff."

She glanced up quickly, her gaze meeting his. Humor danced along the brown of his eyes.

"I was the only person in the place, period. You're messing with me," she said.

"A little. Besides, you clearly picked me up."

Surprisingly, she liked him teasing her. Previous guys either took themselves way too seriously—rebels searching for clues—or they, like her father, took nothing seriously. Life was one big day at an amusement park. No waiting in line, only fun. Nothing subtle like bantering.

"Technically, you made the first move, so I'll have to award the pickup to you." Who knew what the ultimate prize would be for the winner.

He inclined his head as if to accept. Her heartbeat quickened. He wasn't denying his making a move. *Just a man meeting a woman.* It could happen. It could work.

The waitress brought Eric his coffee and her a soft drink. "We have fresh chocolate cheesecake."

Danni sucked in a breath. Cheesecake was one thing she could barely resist. But to enrich it with chocolate…that was almost too low a blow. Could anything be more decadent? Maybe Eric feeding it to her off his fork…

Her mouth began to water.

"Unfortunately, I'm flush out of cash. Just spent my last five dollars," he said.

She glanced his way. His lips were twisting in a smile. "Bring us a slice," she told the waitress. "Put it on my bill. Do you like cheesecake, Eric?" she asked when the waitress hurried away. His name tasted delectable in her mouth.

"I'm not one for sweet things."

That was a point in her favor because she was a lot of things, but sweet wasn't one of them.

"You're a student?" he asked. "I noticed your book."

"I'm going to court reporting school at night. I wait tables during the day. Wednesday is my free day."

"You work at one of the casinos?"

Danni almost coughed. As if she wouldn't immediately be "escorted" out of any casino. "No, a diner. What about you? You mentioned a hotel?"

"I only recently moved to Reno. The company's putting me up in a hotel until I can find my own place."

That explained the corporate haircut. That explained a lot of things.

"What is it that you—" The waitress interrupted

her question when she placed the cheesecake on the table.

How could anyone talk with this tasty bit of heaven between them? Chocolate cookie crust, a scrumptious white chocolate ganache with a dark chocolate spiderweb design. With eager anticipation, Danni took a bite. She immediately closed her eyes and moaned. Ahhh, those spiders were always offering something bad for you. It was the ultimate in chocolate indulgence. The creaminess of the cheesecake melted in her mouth.

"That good, huh?" he asked, his voice tight.

Danni opened her eyes and met his gaze. Oh, yeah, there was fire and heat in his eyes. The only thing that could take her mind off the best tasting thing on the planet was sitting right in front of her. Had she ever been this attracted to a guy this quickly?

"Want a bite?" she asked, her voice turning low and husky.

"Sure."

"I thought you weren't one for sweet things."

"I've changed my mind."

She cut off a portion of her cheesecake and reached across the table. His brown eyes never left hers as his mouth took the chocolate from her fork, his lips touching where hers had been. His gaze became intense as he savored the mouthful. "I could really get used to that," he said.

A shiver ran down her spine. They weren't talking about dessert.

"How is it?" their waitress asked, returning to slide the check facedown on the table toward Danni.

"It's excellent," Danni replied. "Why don't you bring us another piece?"

Eric shook his head, glancing down at his watch. "Actually, I have to go."

Disappointment made the cheesecake lose its flavor. She looked at the waitress. "Bring it to go."

Eric shook his head as if to clear it. An odd tenseness seemed to enter his body. His back seemed more rigid, his hands falling to his sides. "You don't have to do that," he told her. This was no polite I-really-want-you-to kind of refusal.

"No, I want to."

"Thanks," he said, reclining in his seat, the warmth and humor is his eyes gone. What had she done?

So here it was. The brush-off. His body language couldn't be more evident if he'd crossed his arms in front of his chest.

Eric shifted in his chair. And yes, there was the arm cross. Maybe that hot chemistry she felt wasn't mutual at all.

"How about you give me your phone number. I'll call you," Eric said.

His lips were moving, but his actions didn't fit with the words. He made no move to whip out a pen or a piece of paper. She was putting an end to this here and now. In fact, *she* would take the to-go cheesecake, too.

"Listen, I know 'I'll call you' is the male equivalent

of 'let's be friends.' We don't have to go through that scenario."

Eric uncrossed his arms and leaned into the table. There it was again. That sense of danger. That zip of attraction she felt between them. His eyes grew hooded. "I want your number, Danni."

If he'd said I want you naked, on this table, it couldn't have been any less heated than how he'd said he wanted her number. She could feel goose bumps along her arms. And her legs. And even on her ears. He was better than cheesecake.

Against her instinct, she opened her purse and took out a pen and a piece of paper. She also slid Eric's five dollars and enough extra cash to cover the bill, plus tip, onto the table.

"You know what?" he began. "In any other circumstance, I'd hand back a woman's money and use my card. But I'm willing to bet you'd instantly consider me just like every other guy you've met, wouldn't you? Traditional. Boring. So, all right. I'll let you pay for my coffee, and I'm gonna enjoy it."

This man *so* did it for her. After scribbling her name and number onto the paper, she handed it to Eric.

His fingers brushed against hers. She ignored the tingles he gave her with such a simple touch. "That telephone number expires after two days. No waiting to call me to whet my appetite. No game playing. If you want to see me again, you just say so."

Eric took the paper from her and pocketed the number in his shirt. Not a hint of his thoughts regis-

tered on his face. How frustrating. With a nod, she got up and left, walking quickly to her car.

As she slammed the key into the ignition, she realized she'd left the cheesecake behind.

WITH HER LAUNDRY DONE, Danni steered her car toward the highway ready to take the forty-minute drive to Carson City. Wednesday afternoons were reserved for her dad. She owed him that much. Or so he kept reminding her.

The halfway house was a lot better than the visiting rooms courtesy of Nevada's prison system, but since most of her teachers predicted she'd wind up as one of Nevada's "guests" herself, it was no wonder she felt uncomfortable there. That and the fact that any law-enforcement official automatically made her uneasy. Dad said it was in the genes. And some days she believed him.

She found her father tending one of the small gardens at the back of the house. If anyone had bet her a thousand dollars that Daniel Flynn would enjoy getting his hands dirty, she would have upped the ante and called them a sucker.

But she'd be the one paying because her dear old dad had taken a keen interest in horticulture, and she did have to admit, the deep purple flowers he'd coaxed to bloom under the hot Nevada sun thrived. He'd even sent her home with a sack of fresh snap peas once. Yeah, there was another ironic observation there, but it was too hot outside to make it right now.

She dumped her backpack on the ground next to her father. "Hi, Dad. I got the book on plants in dry soils you wanted."

Her father looked up, squinting in the sunlight. "Danielle, my love. That's the first thing you say to me? No, I missed you? Come give your da a kiss."

"Ah, so we're Irish today," she said, good-naturedly.

"Never discount the importance of an authentic-sounding accent. Those of the British Isles are especially good about not sounding cheap. Let's hear your Scottish."

Danni merely shook her head. Growing up, there were Irish Days. Russian Days. Australian Days. All great fun when a person is eight and before men in uniforms with real cop accents knock on the door.

She unfolded the pamphlet she'd stuffed in her back pocket and placed a kiss on his cheek. "This is the information about the horticulture classes at the community college. There's still time to enroll."

"Ahhh, like your dear old ma, trying to set my feet on the straight and narrow path." Her dad's eyes twinkled. After her mother died, those blue eyes of his had led many a woman on the wavy and broad path to sin.

"Just humor me and take the pamphlet."

Her dad took the flyer and stored it in his gardener's bucket. He nodded sadly. "I may have to find legitimate work. With the Internet now, it makes it harder to run a good con. Everybody's a cynic."

"Yeah, that's a real bummer, Dad."

Humor entered her father's famous blue eyes. "Now

that I think about it, something on the Internet might be the ticket."

Danni frowned. "Dad, you're in this halfway house for a reason. It's not supposed to be halfway between jail and crime. It's halfway between you and making straight with your life."

The lightness between them vanished, and a thoughtful look passed across her father's face. "Don't worry about me, Danni-bear. I won't put you through that again."

Silence stretched between them. Seven years they'd been caught by circumstances determined to crush them. The night that had sent each of them on their current course.

Her father stood and clutched her hand. "Come and sit with me under the tree. It's cooler. Tell me what you did today."

He led her to the picnic table some ex-con had thought would be funny to paint in black and white stripes. "Actually, I've met someone."

"You did?"

"His name is Eric Reynolds."

"That name sounds made up," he said, waving his hand.

"Daddy, not everyone's like us. I met him at the laundry. He needed to borrow a dryer sheet."

Daniel Flynn rolled his eyes. "That's weak. Dump him. If a man isn't willing to go to more trouble to impress you, you don't need him."

"I thought so, too. So I charged him a buck."

"There's my girl." Pride laced her father's voice.

"But all he had was a five, so I took all of it. I felt bad about it later, and I ended up buying him a cup of coffee and some cheesecake."

Her father's lips twisted. "Let me get this straight. He got you to buy him a drink, some cheesecake, which by the way I'm surprised you didn't wrestle him for, and dryer sheets?"

"He did pay me for those." And she came close to wrestling him for the cheesecake.

"Did you spend more than five dollars on him?" her father asked, frowning.

"Yes."

"I take it back, it's not weak. He's brilliant."

Danni couldn't help it, she grinned. "Dad, he's not a con man. Not everyone looks at things the way you do."

Daniel sat on the bench. "I don't know why I bother giving you advice. I taught you skills, which you turn your back on, and now you're studying. Studying is bad enough, but what're you studying? Law… It's too painful for me to even finish the thought. Now you're getting taken by a man. Maybe you're more like your mother than I thought."

"And you love me for it," she told him as she gave him a hug.

"More than you'll ever know."

THE PHONE WAS NOT RINGING as she keyed into her apartment. Not a good sign. Had Danni been expecting it to? Hmm, yes, she had.

Hoping, at least.

Dropping her purse by the door, and hooking her keys on the bulletin board, she made a big production of setting the laundry basket on the kitchen table while *not* taking the trouble to see if the red light on her answering machine was flashing. She was not the kind of woman who waited around to see if a man called her.

Still, in the end, she looked at the machine anyway.

The red light was flashing. The muscles between her shoulders tightened. Might not be him. Could be a telemarketer. Could be a charity looking for a donation.

Two messages. Surely one of them was Eric.

"Hi, Danni, it's Cassie. Wanted to see how the coff—"

Skip.

She smiled as the voice of her second caller filled her tiny kitchen. Six words. Six words she replayed at least three times. "I want to see you again."

2

To be honest, Danni wasn't one for dating. From seventeen until twenty the only one-on-one time she'd spent with a male had been with her lawyer. So when other girls her age were learning the rules of dating, refining their flirtation skills, honing their allurement proficiency, she was left alone on her bunk with her notebook.

She'd write for hours in that notebook. Things she wanted to do. Places she wanted to go. She'd developed lists. Lots and lots of lists. The list she reviewed most often was her dodge list. Men she planned to avoid. Ranking near the top of the list were men like her father. That ruled out anyone with charm and a glint in his eyes. Charisma times sexy eyes always equaled a girl in trouble.

Falling right below sweet talkers were the nice boys. First, what in the world could she possibly have in common with them? Nice boys usually came with nice moms, and she'd never pass that test. Plus, they held an aura of boredom.

Next—obviously no one with a criminal past. They'd probably wind up with some kind of one-upmanship thing going on, and that would just be weird.

Anyone wanting to "save" her was also out. Savers usually had more problems than she did, and that was a lot of dysfunction.

Around her nineteenth birthday, Danni realized her list of "not wants" left her with a negative vibe. So she restarted her list to catalog the qualities she wanted. To her surprise, she found she required only three.

Must have a job. Yes, very good start. Very unlike her dad.

Must be driven. Ambition never hurt anyone. Also very unlike her dad.

And be a decent person. That was where Danni always got stuck. Aside from the robbing and stealing, her father was fairly decent. It's not as if he'd go and kick a dog or anything. He did have a code—his code—by which he lived. But she wanted someone, who at his core, had principles. Principles that didn't come with a string of option-out clauses.

So, who did that leave her with? Corporate men and musicians.

She'd struck out royally with the musicians. On the face of it, they seemed to be her ideal. Driven, sort of had a job, and they were sometimes decent, even sensitive. But in the end, their life was all about their music. Their next gig. And could she spot them some money to buy a new amp?

Since the corporate men weren't clamoring at her door to get the girl with a past and a rap sheet, her dating experience had ended there.

Despite him allowing her to pay, Eric seemed cor-

porate. She almost hated to go out with him since this would be her last shot of keeping the corporate fantasy alive. Maybe it would be better to not ever know. If this date failed, where would she be? Did she have the stomach to start her lists all over again? Or never date? Both sounded okay and terrifying at the same time.

Her doorbell rang, and she moved slowly, her fingers stilled on the doorknob. This was it. Her chance to see if corporate worked for her.

She'd told Eric no game-playing, so she opted to be ready on time. He'd told her nice casual. And thank goodness because all the designer stuff was at the dry cleaners. So she greeted him on Sunday evening in black capris and a beaded green tank with a black half-jacket for her shoulders. And she had the shoes right for this play. Sandals, low heel so as not to be too provocative, but strappy to draw attention to her ankles, which for some reason men, be they loser or lawyer, seemed to like.

Her hair had been the problem. She wanted flirtatious and serious. Finally, Danni opted to leave her blond hair down her back with a few strands pulled up in clips.

Appreciation lit his dark eyes, and she let out a relieved breath. She hadn't even realized she'd been nervous. Okay, lie. She just didn't want to admit how very anxious she was. What she needed to do was to openly check him out. Put her focus on Eric.

Actually, he looked a lot better than she remembered. And she remembered him gorgeous. Navy pants,

relaxed enough to be casual, tight enough to let her know he was a man. He didn't appear nervous. Damn.

"You ready?" he asked. She'd forgotten how sexy his voice was, too. Deep and rich and husky.

She nodded, slipping the strap of her spangly purse over her shoulder. "So, where are you taking me?"

He pulled the door shut behind her, turning the handle to make sure it was locked. Then his hand fell to the small of her back. Warmth from his fingers seeped through the thin cotton of her tank.

"One of my coworkers recommended a dinner club. The singer there is amazing."

Was *liking* music a bad sign? "Did you ever want to be a musician?"

He shook his head, and gave her a strange sidelong glance. "No. Why do you ask?"

Danni laughed. "No reason. Never mind." Corporate. Definitely corporate.

Fifteen minutes later they were seated and facing one another as they had at the coffee shop. She sized up the restaurant in moments. Moderate to upper level in price range. Couples mainly. Management probably dealt more in credit cards, not a lot of cash in the till. The real money was probably in the register at the bar. And there was a delicious smell of cheese and artichoke dip in the air.

Hmm, probably assessing where the cash was kept did not indicate ideal first-date behavior. Danni grew ill at ease.

Feeling awkward was a new one for her. As the

roper in her father's schemes, she'd always been highly familiar with her mark, prepared for every situation. Should she approach Eric like that, see him as the mark? Except she hadn't put in the practice time or the research to really know him.

The only advice she had came from Cassie. Her friend's few choice words of wisdom had been to stay with neutral topics. Keep the conversation going. Avoid long silences.

The silence between them now was stretching to near Olympic proportion. She shifted in her seat.

"So tell me, Danni, have you dated much?"

Good Lord, could he tell she was a rookie? Was she that bad at first dates? She'd almost choked on her water.

Eric continued. "You didn't leave me waiting on the couch in your apartment. You haven't asked one hypothetical question, and no coy hair flip."

"Coy hair flip?" she asked, very curious.

"You sort of toss your hair over your shoulder and look at me from the corner of your eye."

As long as he was passing out pointers, she'd give it a try. Danni rotated her shoulders and tossed her hair, never breaking eye contact. "Like this?"

The smile had left his face. "Uh. Exactly like that."

His words were slow, deeper than before. Serious heat burned in his brown eyes.

Maybe corporate was the ticket. No musician had ever looked at her this way. Like he wouldn't mind completely crashing the table between them. And yes, right on schedule, there were the nerves.

Get it together. She couldn't let him get the upper hand. Playing it light should work. Don't make it mean much.

"I have to admit, I haven't dated a lot," she told him, her finger tracing the rim of her glass. She met his gaze. "So tell me more of what I should be doing."

Eric glanced at his watch. "Well, right about now, you're telling me what big muscles I have."

Danni laughed. "So that's what girls normally do then, huh?"

"Yes. Along with wondering how quickly you can get me out of my pants."

Hmm, there was charm. That was bad. Sweet talkers, aka charmers were off her list. But they were so…charming. She'd never associated corporate with charming before. They were supposed to be solid, not whimsical, certainly not witty.

"I thought it was the man who was supposed to be wondering how to get *me* out of *my* pants."

But Eric just smiled, as if he had it all figured out.

The rest of their meal followed a predictable pattern of weather, sports and stuff. She never grew bored though. Her dad had always insisted suits were dull. He believed the nine-to-five life was a drag, and that Flynns were not cut out for the ordinary.

Too soon they'd paid the check and were strolling to the parking lot, toward his car for him to take her home.

Although Danni had limited experience with first dates, she could figure out that him wanting to take her home immediately was not a good sign.

"So that's how first dates go," she said.

"They can," he replied, his voice filled with promise.

"What does that mean?" she asked glancing up. Man, oh man, he was great to look at. She'd kind of avoided it for most of the evening because she knew her eyes would probably want to eat him up like she had that chocolate cheesecake.

"Well, a first date can end here. Or maybe I can say something like, 'Danni, since I'm new in town and don't know what I can do in Reno for fun, do you have any ideas?'"

Danni laughed at his suddenly formal and stiff tone. Yes, that's how she pictured a first date with a corporate suit kind of guy.

"And then you can say…" he prompted.

Fine, Danni understood now how this game worked. She wasn't usually so slow on the uptake, but she chalked it up to her being distracted by his broad shoulders. Or the amazing way he smelled. Or the considerate way he adjusted his longer stride to her shorter steps.

She cleared her throat. "I can say, 'Eric, you haven't lived in Reno if you haven't bowled.'"

The stiffness in Eric's formal posture vanished and he laughed. "Bowling? Are you serious?"

"Hey, in Reno we take our bowling very seriously. And you're no one in Reno if you haven't bowled at least a frame in the Taj Majal of Tenpin."

"And that would be here…in Reno?"

"Right. The National Bowling Stadium."

At the car, Eric held the door open for her, but

blocked her entrance. She turned to face him. His smile was so sexy it hurt to look at. "This I have to see."

If she hadn't been truly aware of the broadness of his shoulders or the strength that simply oozed from him before, she was conscious of it now. Bigness was an angle some con men used to intimidate a mark, so usually she was immune and it certainly never impressed.

But Eric's imposing size made her want to be enfolded in his arms. Feel the strength of him as he pulled her close. Run her fingers along the hard lines of his chest.

He stepped back, his hand seeking hers as he helped her into the front seat, his fingers lightly caressing her hand, arm, shoulder as she slipped into the seat. There was one of those shivers again. Danni had to refrain from fanning her face after Eric shut the passenger door.

The bright lights and the silver plated bowling ball of the National Bowling Stadium soon greeted them. "Never thought I'd see a bowling alley lit up like a casino," Eric said as he angled into a space.

"I told you we take our bowling seriously. Wait until you get inside. You have your choice. You can take the escalator or the glass elevator to the fourth floor."

"By all means, we should take the elevator."

As they stepped off the elevator, Eric let out a low whistle. "You were right. It's impressive."

Over seventy lanes stretched before them. "It's longer than a football field."

Large video screens displaying scores and graphics stood out predominantly. The smell of oil and the

sound of pins hitting the wood surrounded them as they rented some shoes and chose a lane.

"Are you a good bowler?" he asked as they each picked up a ball and checked for the appropriate weight.

"My dad always took an interest in bowling. One of his first jobs was to manually set up pins and send the balls back. The ball returns here over thirty miles an hour."

"Your dad live in Reno?"

Grrr. Why had she mentioned her father? She immediately felt a tension between her and Eric at the mere reference to him. All on her part of course, but surely he could feel it, too.

She shook her head. "No, he never visits here. Stop stalling, you ready?" she asked, infusing breeziness into her voice.

Eric selected a black ball, the first one he'd tried. "Not sure how good I'll do, but I'm ready."

"Remember, the trick is not to try to knock all the pins down on the first roll. Otherwise, the machine cheats you out of your second ball."

He groaned. "And here I've been doing it all wrong. Thanks for the tip."

"You're welcome," she said with a smile.

In fact, Eric turned out to be a pretty decent bowler. While he didn't make any strikes, he managed to clean up with a few spares. Her own approach was lousy, and she sent her ball to the gutter more times than she would have liked. But it wasn't all bad. Every time she bent to retrieve her ball, she felt Eric's brown gaze on her body.

He was checking her out. So she put an extra wiggle in her step. That's when he began missing his spares.

They finished their first game fairly quickly.

"For someone who claims to know a lot about bowling, you don't bowl all that well," Eric teased.

Danni looked up at the screen above their heads. She hadn't even broken a hundred. Pathetic.

"Are you up for another round?" he asked.

"You know, Eric, if I didn't know any better, I'd think you were egging me on just so you could beat me again."

"No, it has everything to do with form."

"Can't tear your eyes off my backside, can you? Okay, I'll give you another game...care to make it interesting?"

Now where had that come from? Had she actually suggested they bet on a bowling game? Old patterns. If he had the chance, her dad bet on which way the wind would blow. And he was always right.

"How about the winner chooses the next outing? And believe me, I won't be choosing bowling," he said, his voice lowered to a provocative timbre.

Next outing? Her stomach got all fluttery. Eric wanted to see her again. She wasn't being a total dud on this date.

Eric stuck out his hand for a shake.

She stood and wrapped her fingers around his strong hand. "It's a deal," she told him. And she wouldn't let the warmth of his hand, or the fact that it took him forever to let go distract her. No she wouldn't. Because she was a professional.

Turning, Danni picked up her ball, blew into the

finger holes and lined up her feet to the left of center. Her ball slammed into the pocket.

Strike.

Strike.

Strike.

"I'm being hustled, aren't I?" Eric asked on the fifth frame.

"Being? Honey, past tense. You *were* hustled." Yeah, old patterns. She hadn't even realized until the sixth frame of their first game that she was deliberately throwing it. It had just been so ingrained.

"We'll see," he vowed. A gleam entered Eric's gorgeous brown eyes. He stepped up and rolled his ball down the lane. All the pins fell on his first ball. Brooklyn style. But a strike was a strike. And he hit two more.

So it seemed she wasn't the only one holding back. It was kind of sweet. It had become fairly obvious in the first few frames of their first game that she was lousy, so Eric had adjusted his own play so he wouldn't blow her out of the water.

Awe. It almost made her feel guilty for what she was about to do. Almost.

Eric was on his approach to get the spare in the ninth frame when the gate suddenly closed and the sweep pushed the remaining two pins away. Eric turned to face her, glaring.

She quickly took a step away from the ball return. She raised her eyebrows in innocence. "Oh, was that *me?* I guess I accidentally pressed the reset button." She added the coy hair flip for emphasis. "Sorry."

His eyes narrowed farther, but his lips were lifting into a wry grin. "Yeah. I can see how that could happen."

Danni finished the tenth frame in a series of three strikes, handily beating Eric. And not a sign of nerves.

He didn't look mad that she'd hustled him. Instead, he seemed almost intrigued. Oh, yes, the theory on nice boys. They liked naughty girls.

"I guess I owe you," he said.

"You can pay your debt with…ice cream."

He sighed heavily. "More time with you. I guess I have to honor my word."

A SHORT WHILE LATER they drove to an ice cream parlor close to many of Reno's casinos, making what she assumed was normal first-date chitchat.

A woman could tell if a man would be a good lover by the kind of ice cream he ordered. Danni actually didn't have an opinion on this, but a theory was forming in her mind.

If Eric chose standard-issue fair—chocolate, vanilla, strawberry—not a lot of adventure between the sheets. Oh, it wouldn't be bad, not as if he ordered something with pineapple topping. That's just yuck. She could never sleep with a man who ordered that. But if a man mixed two flavors she *knew* a little something more would be happening in the sex department.

Eric ordered mega-chocolate peanut butter swirl with nuts and marshmallows. Her nipples got all tingly.

Danni ordered her usual chocolate chip cookie dough and they sat down in one of the booths.

An excited girl in a princess crown danced around her parents' table with her ice cream cone.

Eric laughed. "How long before that scoop of ice cream hits the floor?"

"It won't. She's going to eat the whole thing."

Eric shook his head. "I think you're wrong on this one, ace."

"Care to make it interesting?" she asked. Great. Here she was at it again. She tried to hide her frustration with a smile.

"You're on."

She and Eric watched as the child continued to dance and eat her cone until the very last bite.

Eric turned to Danni. "How did you know?" he asked.

"Because she's a girl and it's ice cream. Dancing in your sparkly tiara is fun and all, but there's a seriousness about dessert that all girls understand."

"Ahhh. So basically you're saying I lost that bet because I'm a man."

"That's exactly what I'm saying. It must be hard to be a step behind all the time. And hey, you didn't tell me the terms of the bet."

"You're right."

She gave him a playful swat on the arm. After they were finished, he helped her to her feet. It was getting late. Just how long could she stretch out this first date? She still wasn't ready for it to end.

"Have you seen the arch yet?" she asked. Reno was famous for the arch proclaiming it to be the Biggest Little City In The World.

"Only by day."

"Well then, you have to see it by night. There's no other way to view it."

Eric drove into one of the casino parking lots and then they walked toward the arch.

"I've heard that if you kiss under the arch you'll have good luck at the tables," she told him. Okay, actually she just made that up, but she was done playing around to see if Eric liked her or not. And if he missed that wide-open invitation, then he was either an idiot or not attracted to her. Which also made him an idiot.

"I don't believe in luck," he said, his tone flat.

She was about to put him in the idiot column, because if anything stuck that her father had taught her, it was that life was a series of luck. Some of it good, a lot of it bad. But most of it luck. Then she realized he was teasing. Despite the darkness, the lights on the strip showed the heat in his eyes. Eric wanted to kiss her. Badly.

"Do you believe in missed opportunities?" she asked, her voice becoming breathless. Because hello, opportunity was knocking.

His stare pinned her in place. "I believe in making my own opportunities."

"Really," she said, her gaze never leaving his. "Well, I wouldn't let you kiss me anyway."

His eyes said *liar*. "I wouldn't want to kiss you. I don't kiss on the first date. What kind of man do you think I am?" he asked as he leaned toward her.

And then suddenly she was in his arms and his lips

were on hers. This was no awkward, first-date-where-do-you-put-your-nose kind of kiss. Eric knew where to put his nose. And his hands. And everything else.

His lips moved along hers slowly. Softly. She'd expected hard, but this, this lightness was amazing. It was driving her crazy.

Her breath caught. His fingers sank into her hair, drawing her closer. His lips firmed, the kiss deepened. His fingers drifted, fanning against her cheek, caressing her.

If she didn't believe in a kiss bringing good luck, she surely would now. She planned to get lucky very soon. Her skin turned sensitive, her nipples tight and aching and every cell in her body chanted *more, more, more.*

All this, and he hadn't even gotten to the good stuff yet. And she sensed Eric had a lot of the good stuff. Mega-chocolate-peanut-butter-swirl-with-nuts-and-marshmallows good stuff.

"You're right, Danni. That arch is something else," he said, his lips lightly tracing along her forehead.

She smiled, not so much from his words, but from the rugged sensuality in Eric's voice that told her he wanted her.

And that's when she got nervous.

Damn. Now he had the power again. She'd never felt so interested in anyone before. That was bad. Very bad.

She *could* throw caution to the wind. After all, for generations people had gambled in this city whether in the silver mining fields, or the casino. One thing she'd learned was to always go after the sure thing,

and Eric Reynolds was not that. The odds were against they'd even make it past date two. They were totally different. They probably wanted totally different things.

It would never work out.

That's when she reached for his chin, drew his lips down to hers and kissed him hard. In the end, she was a gambler.

Although she'd initiated the kiss, Eric quickly took over, backing her into one of the shadowed areas. His tongue swept into her mouth, and she met him kiss for kiss. He tasted faintly of chocolate and peanut butter, and yummy, yummy man. He pulled her to him, his strong arms holding her against the hardness of his chest. His fingers stroked down her arms, finding her hands and placing them around his neck.

He wanted her to touch him. Triumph made her fingers bold. He'd been checking out her backside as they bowled. She hadn't been the only one. Her hands made a winding trail down his shoulders, under his arms and along his spine.

Then she grabbed his ass. There was that gambler side of her again.

With a groan, he broke off the kiss. He rested his forehead against hers, his breathing harsh. "You know, I thought it was bad luck when I forgot my dryer sheets."

"And then you had to deal with me."

"That's when my luck changed."

"I thought you didn't believe in luck."

"Guess that arch made me a believer. I haven't made

out in public since I was in high school," he said, his voice traced with humor and disbelief.

"Glad to see I have a naughty influence on you." Leading someone to a life of sex beat a life of crime any day.

"You wouldn't believe." He paused for a moment, as if deciding what to do next. Taking a deep, almost resigned sounding breath, he reached for her hand. "Come on, let's see how our luck holds out in the casino."

The smile left her face. "No, that's okay. We don't have to go in there."

"I know for a fact you're great with a bet. I'm a wizard with the comps in this place. Let's go."

If it weren't for that mind-numbing kiss, she'd be able to come up with a much better excuse much quicker. But she couldn't step one foot onto that casino floor. It would be all over then. He'd know about her past, and she wasn't ready for that. "No, you shouldn't waste your comps on me."

"I'm teasing. This is where I work."

She stopped. "You work here? At the casino?"

A confused line appeared between his brows as he nodded. "I just started. Is that a problem?"

"I guess I thought it was computers or something."

"I'm head of security."

And that's when Danni hightailed it right out of there.

3

"SO I LEFT HIM on the street. He was there calling my name. Can you believe it?"

If Cassie thought it strange to have Danni knocking on her door after midnight, she didn't show it. Now the two of them sat on the couch waiting for the coffee to percolate. Cassie didn't believe in instant. Or the microwave.

"He almost caught up with me, too, until that cab stopped. Eric even tried to open the door. I never realized how hard it is to flag down a taxi. It was the third one I found."

"Has it occurred to you that being concerned about the person is the normal reaction when that someone you've just lip-locked with flees into the night?"

Danni gave a shudder. *Security.* The word had actually come out of his mouth. "You know, I should have figured it out. He dropped so many clues. He even checked my door to make sure it was locked. How creepy is that?"

Cassie pushed her reading glasses up higher on her nose. "Maybe he wanted to make sure you wouldn't get robbed. Some women might call it thoughtful. Gallant."

"You should have heard him say *security*. Like he was proud of it."

Cassie shook her head. "What are you talking about? Of course he's proud of it. Most people don't have a deep-seated distrust of law enforcement the way you do."

"Boy, I sure know how to pick 'em. *Head* of security, no less."

"Wow, you didn't mention that part. He must be pretty good to be head of security at a major casino."

Eric Reynolds was pretty good at kissing, too. And at touching.

The coffee on the stove began to bubble, so Cassie hopped off the couch. After pulling down two mugs out of the cabinet, she poured Danni and herself a cup each. Cassie was the only person, other than law enforcement and her father, who knew Danni's whole story.

For some reason her best friend seemed to be defending Eric. "He should have admitted he worked in security right from the beginning."

"Danni, would you listen to yourself? You're not even rational. I guarantee you that Eric probably never put 'his job' and 'admitting' in the same category. They don't go together."

Danni just shrugged.

"You like this guy. A lot. What's more, it seems he likes you a lot, too. The only thing that's holding you up is your past. Have you thought that maybe you're using the past as some sort of artificial barrier between you, so you can maintain your feeling of security?"

Danni made the "T" sign with her hands. "Whoa, time out, sister. I hate it when you get all counsely on me. And can we stop saying the word security?"

"Then try you're a woman, he's a man. You both want to hook up. Forget everything else and hook up."

"It's not that easy. Nothing can happen between us." And yeah, it blew because she liked him, he turned her on like no other. That kiss…

"Something can happen between you. You've paid your debt to society. You're not breaking the law. In fact, you're a tax-paying citizen working to make a contribution to the world."

She did pay her taxes now. Weird but true.

Could Cassie be right? Hope surfaced, and Danni had a hard time batting it away. She wouldn't admit to being irrational, but she was quick to make assumptions.

"You told him at the coffee shop that you wouldn't stand for any game playing. I think you should stick to your own rule. Call him tomorrow and tell him the truth."

"I hate the truth," Danni said in a grumble.

"Tomorrow you can come over after you talk to him and we can chat about it all night."

"Who says I'm calling him?"

Cassie sighed. "Let me put this in terms you understand. You're really in a win-win situation. You tell him about your past, he accepts it and you go on to have great sex. You win."

"What's the other win?"

"If he can't get past what happened with your

dad, then he's a jerk and you're better off without him. You win."

Danni sat back against the cushion of the couch. "So, is this what it's like to have grown-up conversations with typical parents?"

"What do you mean?"

"The whole 'You're better off without him. There's other fish in the sea'—all those platitudes come out of people who grew up with a semblance of normalcy. I always wondered who believed that kind of thing."

Cassie laughed, tucking her blond hair behind her ears. "My parents even told me with a straight face."

"Yeah? So did you. Okay, I'll do it. But tomorrow night be prepared for us to trash-talk him because he *will* care. How can someone who enforces law not think about someone who broke it? Repeatedly."

"Always the cynic. How can someone who enforces the law not appreciate someone trying to go straight?"

Danni had no answer for that one.

"See? I'm right and you know it. Come on, you can crash here for the night. I'll drop you off at your apartment in the morning."

Later than evening, Danni fluffed up the pillow on the couch for the twelfth time. Cassie had gone to bed long ago. She'd called her a cynic. What else was new? Although it wasn't so much that she was a cynic, but that she lived in the real world.

Men liked relationships with simple, uncomplicated, low-maintenance women.

And Danni was none of those things.

She closed her eyes and stretched, remembering how good it felt to be with him. For a few hours tonight, she had exactly that with Eric. Uncomplicated, low-maintenance, everything was easy.

What P.T. Barnum had said all those years ago was definitely true. There *was* a sucker born every minute. And right now she was it.

She hadn't thought she could get suckered anymore. That's why it bothered her so much now. Because she wanted something. She wanted something, someone, for the first time.

And cynics knew that as soon as you wanted something, that's the precise moment when lady luck vanished, and you were a goner.

ERIC HIKED UP THE STAIRS two at a time to Danni's apartment, and knocked. No answer. As he'd expected. He'd already done this once tonight.

A woman running down the street away from him was not the usual reaction to his kisses. What the hell had happened?

He'd really thought they'd hit it off. The conversation always flowed. They'd laughed, and that kiss under the arch…it sizzled.

Eric moved away from her apartment door. He saw no light coming from any of the windows or around the doorframe. Her place looked exactly the way they'd left it earlier tonight. Reaching for his cell phone, he dialed her number again.

"I don't know what happened to you tonight, Danni,

but I wanted to make sure you got home safely. I'm sorry if I said anything that upset you. Bye."

That would be his last call to her. He could only try so many times. He'd have a strange story to tell his coworkers when they asked how the date went. He'd have to improvise.

CASSIE WAS THE KIND of person who obviously thought mornings were a time of renewal and happiness that ought to be greeted with a spring in her step and a song on her lips. She also apparently thought mornings began at six, when Danni really knew they should begin closer to ten.

If she looked hard enough she might see small birds chirping gleefully around Cassie's head, reminiscent of Snow White.

Danni pulled the pillow closer. For more than three years while in detention, Danni woke up according to a schedule, to a gong and an abrupt turning on of the lights. The first thing she did after reaching twenty was sleep in.

Cassie, along with her humming, apparently had other ideas.

"Good morning, Sunshine!" Cassie said as she plopped herself down beside Danni on the couch.

"Please, no," Danni grumbled.

"Get up, I made you coffee. You have a busy day. You have a phone call to make."

And that's how Danni found herself four hours later, waiting for Eric. He'd sounded both irritated and

relieved when he heard her voice on the phone. When she offered to give him an explanation in person, he reluctantly agreed to meet her.

Reno's Riverwalk stretched across the downtown area, and wasn't too far from where Eric worked. She could offer to buy him a hot dog from one of the sidewalk vendors. Wasn't there a saying about softening up a man through his stomach?

The Riverwalk area was one of her favorite places in Reno. Something about the trees lining the sidewalk and the sound of the water below made her feel calm. After her years in juvie, she appreciated every chance she had to be in wide-open spaces.

Why had she decided to show up early? Every time a shadow crossed her face, she glanced up to see if it were Eric. Every time it wasn't him, she slumped farther into the chair.

This was a dumb idea. She should have filed this experience under "lost opportunities" and forgotten all about him. Glancing at her watch, she noticed it was ten on the dot. She'd give him five more minutes. No more. No less. She had to study.

A few minutes after ten, Eric walked up to her, appearing tired around the eyes, but oh, so good. The flutters in her stomach returned, and then she remembered that feeling was why she'd sucked up her pride and called him.

Because this was one of the greatest sensations in the world. This mix of anticipation and excitement, with a touch of dread all rolled into one.

Eric appeared very corporate today. Black slacks that hugged his thighs, cotton shirt that only hinted at the muscles of his chest, and a tie. She'd never dated a man with a tie before. And if she didn't angle her play correctly, she might not ever date *this man* with a tie again.

She also noticed the badge he wore on a black lanyard around his neck. He hadn't been wearing it the first time they'd met.

"Hi," she started. "Would you like to take a walk?" she asked, striving for cheerful.

He nodded, but looked none too permanent.

Danni gave a nervous laugh. She could manage the smooth approach. After all, she'd worked on it with her dad since she was a kid. But one glance at the rigid set of Eric's features and she figured he wouldn't be buying smooth. Or any other hustle for that matter.

She'd have to fall back on the truth. Always a last resort.

She led him along the river's path. The large blooming pots of flowers always made her feel welcome in the past. Maybe bringing Eric here had been a mistake. If things didn't work out, her memories of this place would be infected. "You're probably wondering why I ran off like that," she said, sliding her hands along the metal chain lining the walk.

Eric raised a brow. "Not the reaction I'd expect from a woman I've just kissed."

She dropped the chain and reached for his hand. "Oh, Eric, it's not you. You're a great kisser. Totally

off the scale. It's me. I panicked when you suggested we go into the casino."

She'd hoped he'd have joined more in the conversation right about then. That would have made this whole groveling scenario a lot easier. Instead, he stood there…expectant and sexy. Would now be a good time for the coy hair flip?

No. Give it to him straight. She cleared her throat. "Have you heard of a thief named Daniel Flynn?"

Eric shook his head.

"Well, he's been out of the game for a while, so he probably hasn't crossed your radar. He's my father, and he scammed quite a few casinos."

Understanding lit in his brown eyes.

"And I did it with him," she told him slowly.

At that, Eric sat on a nearby bench. His face was still neutral, but his shoulders appeared less tense.

"I've gone straight," she rushed out. "But I wouldn't be welcome in your casino. In fact, I wouldn't be welcome in any casino in any city."

"You out on parole?"

He asked the question in the kind of tone a man *would* get when his date told him she was in the business of cheating people. Kind of a surreal incredulousness.

Danni stared out across the water. "My dad cut a deal. He did extra time, so I was classified as a youthful offender and stayed in juvie until I was twenty."

"Why live in Reno? In Nevada? Seems like temptation would always be in your way."

"That's actually one of the reasons I stayed here. I

wanted to prove to myself I could go straight. Also, the judge in my case took a special interest in me. She's the one who suggested I become a court reporter. I found the proceedings of the court so interesting. If I make the grades, and stay out of trouble, she'll help me find a job."

The tenseness returned to his shoulders. He sat up straighter, and she spotted his pulse beating in his neck. "Have you kept out of trouble?" he asked.

She met his gaze for the first time. She didn't see understanding in his eyes, but maybe the expression of someone wanting to believe her. There was hope again. "Absolutely," she told him quickly. "Listen, I've never spoken to anyone about this before. It's my bad luck you turned out to be in casino security. I'll understand if you can't trust me."

Moments passed. Long, agonizingly silent moments. Danni hadn't known Eric long, but she knew he was envisioning every possible scenario in his mind. She should make it easy on him. They barely knew each other. He didn't owe her anything.

Danni liked him enough to walk away. She dropped his fingers, ready to go.

But Eric wouldn't let her drop his hand. "Come with me," he said.

She was unable to make out his meaning, but he'd extended his hand to her. Another tiny flicker of hope flared. "Where?"

"It's a surprise. Do you trust me?" he asked.

She swallowed and squeezed his hand. "I do." It was

strange trusting someone other than her father and Cassie. But she did, and she felt lighter, freer for it.

"Then come with me."

She followed Eric, shielding her eyes against the harshness of the late-morning sun. In a few turns, she realized they were on a direct path to the casino where he worked.

"What's going on?"

"You say you are around the temptation because you want to prove to yourself·you can go straight. The fact that you ran last night tells me you still don't completely trust yourself." He faced her point-blank. "Since you called me today and told me everything says to me that I can trust you. It's you who's unsure. You don't know whether you can trust yourself. Well, now's your chance."

She glanced at the doors of the casino. Greeters always smiled, but Danni knew they were the first line of any casino's security. "They'll stop me before I take five steps in the place. Those people at the door memorize photos."

"Danni, I know what kind of security measures are in place. Two more days working here, and I would have memorized your photo." He gave her hand a squeeze. "You're with me. It will be fine. Stop stalling. Come inside and prove to yourself you can do it."

"Why? Why are you doing this?" She couldn't keep the wonder out of her voice. No one, no one except maybe Cassie and the judge had ever tried to help her this way.

His brown eyes grew heated. "Maybe I want to see how far I can tip the scale kissing you."

She smiled. A tingle of excitement rushed through her. *Now* was the time for the coy hair flip.

He handed her a twenty-dollar bill. "Come on, prove yourself right."

She glanced at the money, hesitated a moment before she took the bill from his hand. "Thanks for trusting me."

Who'd have thought that having someone's trust was such a turn-on?

They walked together into the casino—loud and filled with activity, even on a Monday. Bells dinged, lights flickered, people alternately cheered and groaned. At one time, this had been home. Not legally, since she wasn't of age then, but of course that hadn't mattered to her father.

"What's your pleasure?" Eric asked. Sure enough, no one had stopped them.

"Poker," she said. "And not Texas Hold 'Em."

"Follow me." He set her up in a chair at a table with quite a bit of action. All amateurs. The loud man who'd already had too much to drink. The retired ladies who were dropped off at the door by a bus. The serious engineer type who'd probably watched the "how to gamble" video up in his hotel room a dozen times.

Easy pickin's.

But not today. In thirty minutes she was done. Sliding off the chair, she found Eric hanging back a few feet away.

"I lost all your money," she admitted.

His eyes burned dark. "I don't care," he replied, staring at her lips.

Her skin burned sensitive and hot. It felt good not even having the urge to cheat. It felt better knowing Eric wanted her.

He nodded toward a hallway that looked as if it led to the administrative offices, and she fell into step beside him.

"So tell me, how would you have cheated back then?" he asked.

Danni scanned the table again. "Easy. Small conservative bets. Just enough to keep the cards flowing and my money going. When I hit a face card, I mark it with my fingernail, or bend the card ever so slightly. Enough times through, I'll have a good idea who has what and bet accordingly. Most people think cheating at cards is all about the right card, and yes, for the most part it is. But don't discount the importance of bet management."

Eric chuckled deep in his throat and the sound shot a thrill to her. "Who'd have thought hearing how you could rob me would be so hot."

"Aha. I've been waiting for that," she told him with a smile. Yes. It was exactly the confirmation she needed to hear. Eric wanted her, like she wanted him.

"You have a problem with men only wanting you for prowess at theft?" he asked, his voice teasing.

"Only from the good boys."

"I'm not so good," he said, his eyes becoming darker.

She had to calm down. While action at the casino table was all well and good, she planned to treat her body to a little Eric action now. She suspected it was a far better rush than cheating at cards.

He unlocked his office and she followed him inside. Her body hummed and she became very aware of the brush of her clothes against her skin.

Not that she'd ever done anything remotely corporate, the room was as she expected it to be. Desk. Executive chair. Two guest chairs.

He sat behind the desk, leaned against his chair. He was a cool one, making her take up the chase. "What is it you wanted to hear?" he asked.

"Confirmation on this theory I have." She perched herself against the polished wood. Forget the chair. Now that she didn't have to work so hard to appear honest and refined, she could allow herself some waviness.

She rested closer to his body, feeling his heat. "My theory is about good boys. That those angelic good boys secretly want the naughty girls. So tell me, Eric, is that one of your fantasies?" she asked, her voice pitching low.

Fire leapt in his eyes as he reached for her, hauling her into his lap, his lips mere inches away from hers. "I'm not feeling particularly angelic right now."

4

HEART-STOPPING anticipation tap-danced on her every available nerve ending. She breathed in his clean, spicy scent. Danni slid off his lap. She wasn't going to make this too easy for him. Otherwise he'd expect everything to be his way. No, not gonna happen.

She took a step, pretending to admire the stuff on his walls, which was practically nothing. He *had* just moved here.

"This is a first for me," she told him over her shoulder, glancing at a nail hole on the pristine corporate shade of light beige. "I've been backroomed, but never officed."

A smile tugged at the corner of his mouth. "Why don't you tell me what being backroomed involves. I want to make sure I'm doing it right."

Turning to face him, she felt her breath catch in her chest. Oh, there was the sexiest glint in his eye. She cleared her throat. "Well, first you need to intimidate me. Usually with your body. Back me up against a wall. That kind of thing."

Eric stood, suddenly seeming bigger and broader than before. He towered above her, and for a moment,

a teeny tiny moment, she felt almost delicate. Yeah, a real shrinking violet she was.

Then he moved toward her. Right into her personal space.

"Like this?" he asked, his voice low and rumbly.

Danni's eyelids grew heavy, and she ached to explore him. "More," she told him.

Even though she was prepared for it, encouraged him, she still took a step backward when he took a step forward. He lifted an eyebrow. Was he goading her?

Damn. Damn. Damn. She didn't yield to backroom bullying. Wait, scratch that. Apparently she did concede defeat to back-office pressure.

But not really. She stifled a moan and lifted an eyebrow right back at him. "That all you got?"

His gaze lowered to the space between them. "It was plenty a moment ago."

"A gentleman wouldn't draw attention to something like that."

His eyes never left hers as he took that final step toward her. This time she held her ground. But it wasn't easy. Before he'd seemed all corporate and fancy coffee at the bistro, but here, alone in his office, Eric was intimidating. But the good kind. She sensed he liked her playing with him, but only to a point. She raised her chin. And winked.

Eric moved, no, he stalked determinedly and the hard wall against her shoulder blades stopped her retreating. Her muscles trembled in excitement.

Okay, it wasn't like she'd really been trying hard to

prevent him. Once again though, she didn't want it to be too easy for him. After all, she was supposed to be explaining the proper backrooming procedure.

Eric looked even better than the night before. His intense brown eyes never dropped her gaze. The ruggedness of his chin, and the breadth of his shoulder…and yes, there it was again. That weird delicate feeling. Her nipples tightened, and her breathing grew shallow. Not her normal reactions to intimidation.

He lowered his head, and she knew in a moment he was going to kiss her. But unlike last night, the idea of kissing Eric seemed very, very scary. And more arousing than anything she'd ever experienced. He knew her secrets, everything about her. She had nothing to hide behind, only honesty and the real her. This didn't feel right. Truth with a man just didn't feel right.

Flip this back into a game.

Okay, sure it was a reverse step in her search for a normal life. She'd made a lot of progress with those visualization exercises counselor Cassie had suggested. But real life was very different. When she ran through those positive mental-visioning drills, nowhere did a highly attractive man she'd allowed to back her up against a wall, figure into the picture. A highly attractive man who showed all the signs that he was about to kiss her.

And yes…what was taking him so long?

Danni licked her lips, and she saw Eric's heated gaze settle onto her tongue. Cheap move. It was an easy way to distract a man. She'd own that.

She made a tsking sound. *Time to get her game on.* "There's no touching in the back room."

Eric straightened, then flashed her a look of disbelief.

"You don't want to violate my rights or anything," she told him formally. Her tone sounded regretful. Not at all how she felt.

"Let me get this straight. In our pretend scenario, I've forcefully detained you, moved you through the casino to a remote, isolated location and *now* I'm supposed to be worried about your rights?" A smile appeared on his lips. "I think you're pulling a con on me."

Now would be a good time for the coy hair flip. But she was in an awkward position with her head leaning against the wall. Instead, she did the next best thing, a side look while saying something innocently suggestive. "Then how will you make me confess?"

Eric's eyes narrowed.

Excellent. She hadn't lost her touch.

Eric raised his arm, placing it above her head. And leaned forward. They stood about as close as two people could stand. Without touching.

She was nearly boxed in. Her only means of escape would be to slip to her right. Challenge lurked in the brown depths of his eyes. If she did try to make a break for it, there was no way she'd make it free. He'd be too quick. So she decided to stay where she was. She folded her arms across her chest, trying to show she was comfortable where she was. A brilliant move, because now the ball had returned to her court with a nice bounce. The power position, right? Didn't feel like it.

Oh, what the hell.

Danni reached up, and pulled Eric's head lower. Their lips touched. At first, he simply stood there, almost in surprise. As if he'd expected her to make some kind of smart-ass remark rather than going for his bod.

Then he joined in, and it was so good. Even though she'd kissed him the one time by the arch, all last night she'd been nervous that she'd never feel like this with Eric again.

Eric Reynolds didn't kiss like an angel. He tasted better than the most sinful of cheesecake. She craved more. He excited her and made her feel special. She wanted to keep that alive for a long, long time.

The hand Eric had braced against the wall lowered to her waist. The warmth of him seeped through to her skin, and she wiggled closer to him. Wanting all of him. His fingers caressed her hip and arousal bloomed inside her.

"Your hands have moved from the wall," she told him, her voice sounding breathless. "Trying to search me?"

"What if I said I had to do a strip search?"

"That's when I'd knee you in the groin."

Eric dropped his hands and laughed. "Aren't you afraid of violating my rights?"

"I'm the detainee. I get to violate all I want. I'm thinking about violating your ear with my tongue right now."

He sucked in a breath and his pupils dilated. Danni grabbed him by the lanyard holding his name badge and tugged on it to bring him to her.

Three seconds of a song emanated from his belt. "What's that?" she asked.

Eric stepped aside and nearly ripped the phone from his waist. He groaned as he looked at the caller ID display. "It's a meeting reminder. Some members of the gaming commission will be here in about ten."

Gaming commission. Great. More law enforcement. The equivalent of dousing her with cold water. "You'll understand if I don't stick around for the introductions."

Eric glanced at his watch, looking tense and frustrated. She couldn't help feeling a little happy about that. She was experiencing her own tension and frustration.

He pressed a kiss to her temple, and she breathed in his scent. Even a quick, totally non-sensual kiss like that made her want him.

"I'll call you when this meeting is over. There are a few other rooms of the casino I'd like to show you," he said.

Now, which rooms did he mean to show her? There were probably over a thousand beds above their heads in the hotel upstairs. Was he suggesting he show her those? Maybe she had this whole nice guy thing wrong. Maybe, deep down, all guys hid a naughty side.

An image of him naked and tangled in sheets flashed through her mind.

And maybe that wasn't so bad. This was a theory she'd enjoy exploring.

"The Chinese restaurant makes great noodles," he suggested with a wink, as if he knew what she'd been thinking.

But her assessment was right. Very naughty—tempting a woman with carbs.

He'd donned a suit jacket before opening the door to his office. When had she ever thought a man in a suit and tie could be boring? Now she knew that particular garment hid muscles and heat. Eric walked with her to the front door of the casino. Fully corporate now.

Danni's cell phone rang as he put her into a cab and prepaid the driver. Cassie. It wasn't like her to call in the middle of the day when she had so many patient appointments. Cassie's relationship and marriage counseling practice had really grown. But then they'd both come a long way since that first meeting when Danni was twenty and approaching her release date from detention. Cassie had been a volunteer counselor donating hours of her time to talk and listen. Her help eased the transition into society for the young women, like Danni, who'd spent much of their time behind bars. They'd grown into lifelong friends.

Danni flipped open her phone. "Hello?"

"You're not in class, good, I need you to meet me in my office. I've canceled all my appointments for the rest of the day."

"Canceled? You? I don't believe this. Are you okay?" Danni's heart rate picked up in anxiety for her friend. Professionalism and Cassie were practically the same word. She lived for her patients. Danni couldn't even imagine a scenario where she'd stand them up. "How many of your limbs are bleeding?"

Cassie groaned loud and clear even with Danni's

crummy cell phone reception. "If only I were bleeding. Come quick."

Eric leaned into the car. "There a problem?" he asked after Danni hung up the phone. Concern lit his eyes.

"I don't know. Cassie sounded pretty upset. And she's not one to overreact to trouble."

Now his eyes narrowed. "What kind of trouble? Maybe you shouldn't involve yourself with this."

For a moment Danni didn't understand why Eric seemed so worried. Her best friend was in trouble. Of course she'd get involved. Then she realized Eric thought the trouble might be of the illegal variety. She quickly smiled. "Don't worry. Cassie is someone I met after juvie. Believe me, she's as straight and narrow as they come. Almost squarer than you," she teased him.

"I'll refute that square remark later," he promised, and oh yeah, did that sound good. He shut the door and she just knew he'd stay on the curb until her car disappeared from sight.

She forced herself not to turn around to verify. It was her gut that told her looking back would shift the power back to him. So her fingers dug into the blue cotton of her skirt. Danni knew she must have a stupid grin on her face. The cab was now almost beyond the casino.

Maybe one look wouldn't hurt? She twisted in her seat. Oh, yeah. Eric still waited there. She couldn't read anything in his neutral expression or the way he'd stuffed his hands into his pockets. He gave her a curt nod and she quickly twisted around in her seat, stupid grin even wider.

ERIC WATCHED DANNI'S CAB merge into traffic. Twice in two days he'd watched her get into a cab and leave him. But this time was infinitely better.

This time she looked back.

She'd confessed to a past. He hadn't expected that. Oh, he'd anticipated some kind of explanation for her unusual behavior last night, but the simple truth Danni offered with that hint of vulnerability got to him.

He smiled as he shook his head. People didn't get to him. They never had. He skirted around a few tourists looking at a map outside the entrance to the casino. Nodding to the guards at the front door, he made his way to the administrative areas. He hadn't been giving Danni the brush-off with that story of a ten a.m. meeting; his superiors *were* expecting a progress report. A progress report that was waiting for him in his office.

The casino held an air of excitement and hope, and he had to weave his way around a multitude of tables and machines. The gaming floor was not designed to give a person a direct route to the restaurants, doors or elevators leading up to the hotel rooms. Eric had to pass by every conceivable kind of temptation. Funny that with all the decadence and enticements surrounding him, Danni had proved to be the biggest lure.

After unlocking his office, he cut a glance to the wall where he'd pinned her delightful body. *His* body remembered everything. The softness of her hair against his cheek. The weight of her breasts against his chest. Damn if he couldn't still hear that sexy intake

of breath she'd made when his fingers caressed the curve of her hip. Yes, things between them were definitely back on track.

He hadn't calculated on sex coming up so soon in their relationship. Although he'd been charged with overplanning and being far from spontaneous, Eric usually won over any sex partner with his deliberate and intentional approach to sex. In fact, he savored the chase…the anticipation.

But with Danni, he wanted to rip her clothes off and have her right there against the wall. He didn't want to chase. He didn't want to anticipate. What was wrong with him? He closed his eyes and focused. Focused until every thought of Danni faded into a controllable compartment in his mind.

Ex-girlfriends accused him of being shut off, or hiding from some kind of emotional trauma in his past. The truth was far less dramatic. No childhood pain hid in his closet. He was simply a loner. He didn't have to get involved.

This was reason number one that made him good at his job.

Danni had proven to be unpredictable. That's why it had taken him a moment to recover from her admission of her old ways. Offering her that twenty bucks had come from the hip. He hated shooting from the hip. Planning and execution was his forte.

Another reason he was good at his job.

Grabbing files from his desk, he headed out of the building. He wasn't in top form for this meeting. Sure,

he had good things to report, but after that tossing and turning in his bed last night, he'd finally given up the pretense of trying to sleep. Instead he hit the gym around four-thirty to work out his frustrations.

With thoughts of Danni, a different set of frustrations flooded him. Maybe he'd have to hit the gym again. He wanted her. Wanted her with the single-minded determination he usually reserved for work. But why?

Danni had a wariness, a cynicism that drew him to her. Yet she was a woman with a lot to prove. Eric admired that about her. But had she set out to prove that his faith in her wasn't wasted?

He winced at the thought. Then once again, he pushed the idea of Danni out of his mind. There were a lot of people counting on him. He had a job to do as well. He wouldn't fail.

TWENTY MINUTES LATER, Danni stood outside Cassie's office. Her best friend met her at the locked door. Not even Cassie's receptionist hovered around the place.

When Danni saw her best friend, all remnants of her goofy grin vanished. Cassie's skin stretched tight across her face with strain, and she was reaching for her glasses. A nervous habit that still existed, even though she'd gotten that laser procedure a few months ago. "Follow me," Cassie said. "It's on my computer."

Danni followed Cassie down the hall, then halted with a gasp.

For years, Cassie had advocated a "no computer"

policy for her desk. Something about being cluttered and distracting from real work. With her practice expanding, the small closet she'd used to house her computer was now stocked with large file drawers and the computer now sat on her desk. A computer that flashed two very naked, very into each other and very entwined people.

"You doing research on Internet porn?" Danni asked, grasping for a reason those writhing images would now be bombarding her. Somehow the porn stuff didn't seem to mesh with the avocado-green of Cassie's walls. Cassie insisted it was a calm, soothing hue great for her patients that would soon be the next "in" color. Basically, it reminded Danni of her grandmother's kitchen back in Oklahoma.

"Look closer," Cassie insisted, her voice tight.

Danni sat in the comfortable brown chair and studied the action on Cassie's monitor. Then she tilted her head sideways. First right. Then left. "Is that his…what is that?"

Cassie made a groaning noise. "You don't want to know."

Danni swiveled on the computer chair to stare at her friend. "Then why am I looking at this?"

"Because I need an honest opinion. Can you tell that's me?" Cassie asked, scrubbing her hand down her face.

No way. No way in hell. Danni's eyes widened, but she quickly spun around to take another peek. "Oh, you weren't a blonde yet. Now I can tell it's you."

Cassie groaned again. "So if I hadn't told you, would you be able to recognize that it's me?"

"Do you want me to lie? I'm really convincing, you know." The couple shifted on the bed. "What's that thing he's doing right there?"

Cassie made a choking sound. "That's his special move."

Danni couldn't look at the screen another second. She frantically searched around the office to distract herself from the monitor. Hmm, when did Cassie get that new picture on the wall? What was that…a blue dog?

She'd never had an awkward moment with Cassie. Ever. The woman knew every embarrassing intimate detail of Danni's life, including the details of her first time, which had been on top a hay bale. But this, *this* was awkward.

Loud moans from the monitor filled the room. Danni almost choked. "Well, at least you were enjoying it."

Cassie rolled her eyes. "Oh, come on," she said, sounding exasperated and stressed. "I was faking it. Look at him."

Danni was trying not to.

"What he lacked in skill," Cassie went on, "he definitely made up for in enthusiasm. Watch him just pound away."

Again, Danni was trying not to.

"Actually, it was pretty sweet," Cassie said, her voice turning softer. "He wanted me to come so hard, he was really trying. Hence all the moaning."

"So you're pretending?"

Cassie took her eyes from the screen for the first time and met Danni's gaze. "It's *called* faking. Don't you do it?"

"No. How's the man ever going to know what you like if you don't tell him? Doesn't pretending just confuse them?"

"We were twenty. We'd been together since we were about eight. Our whole life was mapped out. We were saving ourselves for each other."

Another loud moan came from the monitor. "So what made you two change your minds?"

"Obviously some guy never talked you into playing 'just the tip,'" Cassie said, the smile on her face not reaching her eyes.

"Yeah, I guess there were some good things about being incarcerated during the hormone years." However, that might also account for the hay bale—trying to capture something she'd missed out on. "So you…lie? The most intimate act between two people and you lie through the whole thing?" Danni asked.

Cassie hissed a breath, ruffling her straight blond hair. "You've never added in an extra moan, just to, you know…wrap it up?"

"No. Never." Once again this proved the warping of her education. Honest people lied in bed, while the liars didn't? Go figure.

Danni snapped her fingers. "You know, this explains a lot now that I think about it. Remember that one guy I dated. Ken. He really sucked in bed, but he thought

he was a god. I'm sure it was this whole faking business. There should be a rule. It gives men the wrong idea of what they should be doing. He thought *I* had a problem."

Cassie shrugged. "Sometimes I have things to do."

"Well, it could be worse." In Danni's experience it could always be worse. And she had a real skill at finding the brighter side.

"How?"

"At least your time on film is with someone good-looking. He's got a great ass."

"Yeah," she said with a sigh.

Something in Cassie's voice, that wistful tone made Danni pause. And suddenly it all clicked. *This* was the guy. The man who set Cassie on the path to learning as much about herself as possible and then spreading that to everyone else around.

"He's the one, right?" Danni asked.

Cassie stiffened, instantly returning to counselor persona. "I don't know what you mean."

Wow, this was weird. Danni had never seen Cassie even remotely flustered. She even had her arms folded across her chest. Protectively.

Oh, sure it was okay to show your best friend the illicit sex tape, now Internet video podcast that everyone could see, which you made when you were young and stupid, but talk about the man in said illicit sex tape…

A good friend wouldn't press the issue. Delve deeper. But then most people weren't best friends with

the woman who wrote *How Could I Have Made Such a Mistake?—How To Have Mature, Adult Relationships While Still Hating the One Who Broke Your Heart.*

Most people didn't view avoidance as a four-letter word like Cassie did. Cassie had led Danni down the rocky and often painful path of self-discovery. It was only right of her to return the favor. And just what was Cassie's catch phrase? A smile played on Danni's lips. Ah yes, she remembered. Identify. Rectify.

It was time for Cassie to start identifying. Or at least dishing the dirt.

"How'd you find this?"

"My sister sent me the link. I'm not even going to ask her why she was on this site."

"So, who's the guy?" Danni asked again, her tone firm.

"Oh, the one who's going to meet the business end of my heel? Doesn't matter."

Danni hid a grin. Weak attempt at diversion from the question. That must be the problem with living a life of self-truth. When you didn't want to tell the truth, you didn't have the skills to lie.

"Cassie, come on."

Cassie hesitated a moment, as if even saying his name would make her head start to spin. "His name is Dirk. Dirk the soon to be dead."

Danni laughed.

"What's so funny?"

"Nothing, I mean it's the name. I've heard it before,

but never knew anyone in real life was called Dirk. Do you ever see him?"

"Dirk called me a couple of times after his *period of discovery,* but I wasn't interested. His mom still lives in my hometown, so unfortunately I bump into him at every major holiday."

Danni was now certain there was a story here, and she couldn't wait to get to the good part. She opened her mouth to ask another question. However, Cassie was already talking.

"I'll tell you one thing. Holidays will be a joy after this, because I'm going to find whatever computer he used to upload this thing and smack him in the face with it."

5

"I HAVE A DATE TONIGHT after class," Danni told Cassie, reaching for her cell phone. "Just let me call and cancel."

Instant regret filled Cassie. "What? No. You're not going to cancel a date because of me. I can't even believe you would suggest that."

For the first time since she'd met Danni, her friend seemed to be going out with someone semi-normal, while at the same time Danni had managed to tell the man the truth about her past. Cassie wasn't about to let her blow it.

Personal crisis or not, she and Danni had worked long and hard to get to this point. Despite Danni's natural inclination to ruin her own life, Cassie wasn't going to let her wreck it on *her* watch.

Danni hesitated, phone midway to her ear. "You're upset. I—"

"It's against the rules," Cassie said, cutting her off.

Danni's brows drew together in obvious confusion. "Rules? There are rules about breaking a date?"

"Certainly," Cassie sighed. "Sometimes I forget you didn't learn the same things at fifteen that I did."

"Rules. Rules. Rules. Is there anything in my life that doesn't have a rule?"

Cassie looked at Danni, expressionless. "No, there are always rules. So listen closely. When you have a date, the previous plans with your girlfriends take the back seat."

"I thought the rule was never cancel plans with your girlfriends for a boy. Doesn't that seem more empowering?"

"I don't know what you're talking about." Cassie shrugged. "That's just the way things are."

Danni traced her finger over the plastic case of her cell phone. "But I can't believe you'd even suggest I go out with someone right now."

Cassie unfolded then folded her arms across her chest, her expression fierce she knew. She couldn't help it, and she didn't really care. "You know, now that you mention it, I'm feeling a definite all-men-are-scum sentiment right now. Maybe hanging out with me would save you from one more really scummy man."

Danni's gaze dropped, and she looked at her nails. Over the years, Cassie had learned to pick up the many subtle hints and gestures of the woman who strenuously guarded her every inner feeling and emotion. It was so obvious Danni would rather be with Eric. And yet she wouldn't hesitate to break her date to help Cassie. That's what made Danni such a good friend. Eric was the future. Cassie's problems with Dirk were the past. If Cassie wanted to get one message across

in her writings and work with patients, it was progress
never went backwards.

Cassie reached for Danni's shoulder and gave her a
squeeze. "Really, don't worry about it. I'm *embracing
the calm* even as we speak." Cassie made a big show
of taking a deep breath and letting it out slowly. "But
I do need your help. How do I locate a guy without
asking his mother for the address?"

A sly smile lit Danni's face. "Ahhh, finally. I can
actually contribute."

Cassie arched a brow. "How about finding someone
to rough the guy up?"

The color drained from Danni's face. "Uh, I probably
know someone, hmm, maybe someone from—"

Cassie decided to give her friend a break and waved
her hands through the air. "I was kidding. Why is it you
never get my jokes?"

"Maybe because they aren't funny," her friend said
with a wink, the color returning to her face.

"I'm a riot in the Marriage and Relationship
Therapy community."

Danni nodded. "I'm sure you are. Now listen, I'm
about to impart a few rules of my own. First, for every
five-minute con, there's hours of investigation."

"Do we run a credit check? Internet search? Look
at the ISP for whoever linked the tape?" Cassie's questions came rapid-fire.

"Call his old telephone number," Danni suggested.

Cassie's shoulders slumped in disappointment.
"That seems so, so simplistic."

"It always is. TV and movies always make the basics so outlandish. You wouldn't believe what kind of information people volunteer over the phone. Like their weight, social security number. You name it."

Cassie picked up the receiver of her multi-line telephone on her desk, and began to dial. It really irked her that she still knew Dirk's old home phone number by heart. Suddenly she was seventeen again, dialing this number nervously after school. Aching for him to be home from football practice. Almost hoping that he wasn't.

Danni gave her the thumbs-up sign.

Her heartbeat quickened as the connection went through. She'd expected to hear Dirk's mother's voice, but Dirk answered. Two rings. Two lousy rings and she was now ear to mouth with the demon spawn himself. Her stomach tensed with nerves.

"Hello," he said, his voice deeper. Smooth and sexy.

Cassie slammed the phone down. "He's there."

"So he answered, and then you…hung up?" Danni asked, looking as if she was trying to hide a smile.

"Yes. Figures he'd be back in Carson City. We'd planned that he would become an architect and join his father's construction firm after college. I guess he stuck to the plan. Except for the me part." Heartbreaking rat. Heartbreaking rat with a computer.

Danni shrugged her shoulders. "Now you know where he is."

A moment later the phone began to ring. Cassie

peered at the display and groaned. "Oh, no. I can't believe it. That's a Carson City exchange."

Danni sucked in a breath. "He must have star-sixty-nined you. Sorry, I haven't done a lot of the covert stuff since all the new phone options. Are you going to answer it?"

"No. Yes. I am a mature adult woman. I can handle this." Cassie snatched the receiver from the bed. "Hello," she barked into the phone.

A long pause was her answer. Then… "Cassie? Cassie Coleman, is that you?"

Every atom, no smaller than that, was charging right now. The voice on the other end was definitely Dirk Carr. More resonant and sexier, but yes, still the scumbag of her dreams.

"Yes. Who is this?" she asked, feigning polite bewilderment.

"It's Dirk Carr. You just called me."

She snatched a pencil off her desk and worked it between her fingers. "Oh, right," she said, shooting for casual. "Well, I'm glad you called, Dirk. I've been needing to talk to you."

Excellent. She made it sound as if he'd been the one to call and she'd said need, not want. "I was planning on driving up to Carson today. When would be a good time for you?" It would take her less than an hour to drive to her hometown, and she'd like to get this taken care of now. It's exactly like what she wrote in her book—*no putting off when putting together your life.*

"Anytime," he said, sounding open and warm. "I'm

living in Carson City now. I was helping my mom move some stuff when you called before."

"I'd heard she'd broken her knee a few months ago. How's she doing?" Bad move. She did *not* want to make this personal.

"Oh, she'll be skiing soon enough." His rich voice held laughter. "Let me know when you get here and I'll take you to dinner."

She was about to tell him what they needed to talk about, but then she thought of the dinner bill she could run up on his dime. Appetizer. Dessert. The steak and lobster special. Wine. How could she forget about the wine? Maybe a coffee, no, a latte, afterwards.

She tamped down her barely-there feelings of guilt. No way. Her bare boobs were on computer screens all over the world, and her Dutch treat days with Dirk were over.

"Sounds good," she said with an evil smile.

"And Cassie, I'm looking forward to seeing you again." His voice dipped lower, and every hormone in her body responded with a jump. Just like always.

When that sensation trickled down her spine, she slammed the phone into the receiver. Picked it up once more and slammed it again. There'd be no playing "You hang up," "No, *you* hang up" games with him as they had at fourteen. Good thing she hadn't used her cell phone. Not as much satisfaction in depressing a button.

"What happened to embrace the calm?" Danni asked.

"Oh, screw the calm. Calm is overrated. Revenge. Castration."

"WHERE ARE WE GOING?"

Eric just laughed. "It's a secret."

"Oh, come on," Danni urged him. Strange. For a woman whose life had been built around secrets, she sure didn't like it when they were kept from her. Her heart beat faster in anticipation and her skin felt more sensitive.

He gave her a sideways glance. "I will tell you it's not bowling," he said dryly, but she saw the humor lurking in the brown sexiness of his eyes.

Danni laughed, but she was determined to ferret out his secret.

Curiosity was a fault. A fault all Flynns seemed to share, but must suppress. Her back suddenly stiffened as the cautionary voice of her father filled her head. She had a lot of questions where Eric was concerned, yet as her father always warned, curiosity was a dangerous thing. It made you less careful because you stopped following the plan. Recklessness sent out clues. Got you caught.

However, she wasn't on the grift with Eric. She was nothing other than honest. An anomaly with a Flynn for sure, but one that felt right. And so did curiosity. Judging by Eric's pin-her-against-the-wall response earlier, he wasn't immune to her charms. Maybe she could seduce their destination out of him.

Her body instantly liked that idea. Her nipples tightened.

She glanced down at her jean-clad legs and running shoes. Not seduction material. A side-slit clingy skirt

was the better uniform for a little erotic persuasion. A Flynn's real skills rested in creating a mood, an illusion to where a mark felt comfortable and willing to share anything from the location of a security camera to access codes. But she couldn't do anything like that, looking like someone more apt to help a person move boxes to their new apartment. Eric held all the cards.

"So, you're really not going to tell me?" she asked, infusing just the right touch of playful and offhand into her voice.

He shook his head.

Yeah, you can keep your secret Mr. Security Man. She shifted her focus to the desert outside the window.

"So what happened with your friend?" he asked after a moment.

Danni twisted in her seat toward Eric. "I've never, ever seen Cassie so flustered, so...so...not herself. She is the most put together person I've ever met. It's like she's completely without dysfunction." And she went on, telling Eric most of the story, leaving out the embarrassing parts.

Wait a minute...did he just sidestep? Change the subject? Divert her attention to something else? She'd been determined to find out where he was taking her. Then with one quick question from him, she'd spent the next five minutes talking about Cassie and her problems.

Danni glanced quickly at Eric. Corporate. His long fingers steady around the steering wheel.

Great brown eyes. Unangelic kissing. And apparently a man who liked his secrets.

"Guess it's no surprise Cassie would lose it because of a man," she said rather quietly, because Danni herself had lost every inkling of knowledge about human nature with Eric. She was playing this all wrong.

"Would you lose it over a man?" Eric asked, his tone curious.

"Absolutely not."

"Good, I wouldn't want you to."

She met his eyes then. A strange coldness rested in the once-warm depths. Again she got the feeling that Eric liked his secrets.

"We're here," he said as he signaled their turn.

Danni glanced toward the large wooden sign featuring a lot of shiny golden glitter. To be honest, she'd been tempted in the past to "find her fortune" at the Golden Dig, a tourist trap outside Reno. "We're panning for gold?" she asked as they got out of the car.

"Thought you might like trying to earn it an honest way," he said with a wink.

"Where's the fun in that?"

Eric laughed as his hand slid to the small of her back. Ohh, she loved when he did that. Musicians and con men didn't curve their hand along a woman's back, giving her that warm protected feeling. Who knew she wanted that feeling?

The establishment exuded an atmosphere reminiscent of the mining towns that quickly popped up all over Nevada and California once gold was discovered.

From the wooden sidewalks and the broken-down wagon in the middle of "Main Street" to the water pump and horse ties outside the planked wood mercantile, the whole place had the kind of tourist kitsch that begged cynicism from a Flynn. Might not be totally historically accurate, but it was definitely campy fun. Danni loved it on sight.

"Do you know how to do this?" she asked, trying to distract herself from Eric's closeness.

"I already have our claim staked. At least for the next two hours." He pointed toward a small area by the river, which was a short distance from the parking lot. He took a few steps ahead of her, then reached back lifting his hand to hers, helping her down the incline.

She could have easily hiked down that hill to the riverbank. Heck, hike was too big a word for the gentle slope down to the water. After all, she could schlep a loser boyfriend's guitar amp with no problem. But something about having a sexy man offer his hand made every cynical instinct she had want to sing songs about starshine in the morning.

So Danni grasped his hand, let him lead her down the rise and embraced the feelings of girly delicateness invading her limbs.

Eric dropped her hand when they reached the bank and began to take off his shoes.

She made a tsking sound with her tongue. "Second date and you're already stripping," she told him. "Anyone ever tell you you're easy?"

"Play your cards right, and you might see me take off a lot more."

"I know how to play *all* the cards," she reminded him. Visions of Eric doing away with a lot more clothing began bombarding her already intrigued senses. Chest hair or not? Boxers or briefs? Tattoos or piercings? Wait, she could probably answer that without any clothing removal. Corporate and tattoos didn't mix. Yet, wouldn't it be cool and surprising if he did?

"Maybe that's what I'm counting on," he said.

She'd read somewhere that a woman subconsciously decided to make love to a man within fifteen seconds of interaction. Suddenly the decision her subconscious had made several days ago asserted itself because anticipation was exactly what she felt.

It wouldn't be today. Probably not tomorrow. This was a slow-burning seduction. But she *would* be making love with Eric, and her body…no, *she* couldn't wait for the heated weight of his body along hers. That frenzied need to remove his clothes. The urgency of his fingers against her skin.

She sucked in a breath. Her muscles were already relaxing and her blood pumping in expectancy. Except now was not the time. She didn't want this fast.

Danni kicked off her shoes, and slipped off her socks, sticking them inside. She hadn't expected to be showing off her naked toes quite so soon in their relationship. She snuck a quick peek at her feet. Not so bad, the pink polish she'd managed to get on two days

before still appeared okay. She rolled up her jeans to below her knees, then turned to glance at Eric.

Was there a part on the man's body that looked bad? Certainly none of the body parts she'd viewed so far. And his muscular lower legs with the right amount of sun were no exception. Not even a weird pinky toe.

Not that she was complaining. In fact, if he planned to show off more body parts, she wouldn't shy away.

"Ready?" he asked, extending his hand toward her once more and helping her to her feet.

"Yes," she said, breathless.

The sand felt warm and soft beneath her toes. Eric grabbed two pans, handing her one. "Scoop the sand, fill it with water and sift. Easy as that," he explained.

"Now you're talking like a con man."

"When things are right, they *can* be that easy."

She glanced at him sharply, but he was already bending over, catching water and sand into his pan.

Being with Eric was that easy. No need to hide behind pretense. Or plans. Everything flowed naturally.

She'd just ignore that shiver of alarm that raced through her body.

6

AT THE SILVER MOON, Dirk stood when he saw Cassie approaching the table. His blue eyes widened, then narrowed. In desire.

Score.

"I love it when you wear your hair all down your back." "You look so hot in blue." "Mmm, you smell great." That was one of the good things about teenage boys, they told you exactly what turned them on.

Meanwhile, teenage girls in love remembered everything. Women could use that knowledge to their advantage.

Hair curly and down her back. Check.

Blue sleeveless dress with heels. Check.

The flowery soap she had used in high school. Check.

She'd armed herself fully. What she hadn't counted on, however, was that he'd be sporting quite an arsenal himself. He'd been lean and lanky in high school, but his shoulders had filled out beautifully. In fact, all of him looked pretty stunning.

And that smile, that gorgeous smile of his that never failed to bring her to her knees and send her away from whatever sensible path she knew she should walk.

Her lips curved in a smile all for him.

No, of course she didn't need to study.

Ditching sixth hour sounded great.

Yeah, why not film their love?

Her smile instantly vanished. Her fists clenched at her sides.

Dirk Carr, you are going to pay for every moment of humiliation I have suffered at your hands.

Excellent. Despite her current situation, she'd set a goal for herself. She was well on her way to a *Daily Change,* as she advised in her book, and broke up what appeared to be insurmountable transformations into smaller goals a woman could challenge herself with every day. By already identifying an objective and stating her intention, steps one and two were complete.

Feeling good about that, Cassie allowed Dirk to pull out her chair. Except she ended up brushing against his now very broad chest. The heat from his body was overwhelming.

Perfectly natural, she cautioned herself. After all, he had been her first lover.

The waiter appeared out of nowhere and handed her a menu. Or maybe he'd been there all along, hovering, and she'd been too engrossed in Dirk's stupid chest. "Would you like an appetizer?" the waiter asked.

And onto step three—actualizing. "Shrimp cocktail," she answered without opening her menu.

"Six or twelve?" the waiter asked.

"Do you have anything bigger?"

The waiter looked uncertain. "I could double the twelve."

"Why don't you triple," she told him with a delighted smile, then looked around the restaurant. Anything to avoid Dirk's now penetrating stare.

The Silver Moon was where Dirk had taken her to eat the night of the prom. If anything, it was even more elegant than she remembered. Figured. She'd really only had eyes for him at the time. Dark cherry wood paneling lent an intimate atmosphere. Everything from the gorgeous crystal chandeliers to the flickering candles on the pristine white tablecloths shouted sophistication and expense. And romance.

Why had he suggested this place?

Dirk had taken his lunch to school every day for a month in order to save enough money to take her here. Of course it wouldn't have mattered, they could have eaten peanut butter and jelly sandwiches on the hood of his car and she'd have been just as happy, she had loved him so much.

Her fists clenched again, and she shook them out under the table. He'd better start saving his pennies in a hurry, because tonight's meal would not come cheap.

"You look amazing, Cassie."

Cassie had to glance at him after that proclamation. She'd always found him gorgeous, his short blond hair, straight jaw, sexy full lips. There was the hand clenching again.

She would have been flattered by his compliment,

but then she remembered how she looked bare-ass naked on the computer in her office. Thanks to him.

"Bring a bottle of the Cabernet Sauvignon please," she told the waiter as he brought them glasses of ice water.

"Are we celebrating something, madam?" asked the waiter.

Oh, if only he knew. Back when she lived here, The Silver Moon was *the* place in town to celebrate. Anniversaries. Engagements. Telling off the jerk who posted your sex tape on the Internet. "Yes," she told the waiter, not elaborating further.

Dirk didn't bat an eyebrow at her ordering a seventy-five-dollar bottle of wine. In fact, he looked relaxed and downright happy sitting casually against the high-backed mahogany chair. Clearly she'd have to ramp it up a bit.

"It's good to see you again. I can't tell you how many times I've thought about you over the years," he said, his smile genuine.

Something twisted in her heart at the sight of that mouth. At the rush of aching memories and hunger, Cassie eyed her water glass. If she threw the contents in his face now, she'd have to leave before she ordered the steak special. That had to be at least thirty bucks. She gave Dirk a tight smirk instead.

"Congratulations on your book, by the way. Everyone here is so impressed with what you've done. Me, too," he said. His voice was rich and sexy and warm, the realness behind his words clear.

Cassie hated that he was being pleasant. He was

taking all the fun out of this. She wasn't sure she'd be able to handle a whole evening of him being nice to her.

Singing and a flaming dessert caught her eye. A waiter was serenading a beautiful love song in Italian to the hand-holding couple at the next table. "Happy Anniversary," the man announced, loud enough for everyone to hear.

The woman blushed. "Oh, you shouldn't have done this, Chris."

The man kissed her hand.

Cassie almost rolled her eyes.

She spotted their waiter. Strike that. There was no "their." *Her* waiter. She spotted her waiter returning to the table. Oh good, her shrimp had arrived. If she could order quickly, she might be able to salvage something before Dirk stalked off into the night after she told him what a jerk he was for uploading that tape.

And that he was bad in bed.

Wait a minute. If *he* stalked off, *she* might get stuck with the bill.

"I was surprised when you called. I didn't think I'd ever hear from you. Not after that Labor Day party at Jake's house," he said, watching her intently.

Ah yes, he'd tried to corner her in the kitchen. Tried to get back with her. Standing across from him, Jake's family's dinette between them, she'd finally come up with the title of her book. It was natural for humans to make mistakes. So she planned to only make better ones. Not getting back with Dirk would be one of those.

Did he sound flattered? Expensive meal or not, she simply could not sit here and let him think she *wanted* to contact him. Be pleased about it.

"I never intended to," she said, reaching for a shrimp and dipping it into the cocktail sauce. Just thirty-five more to go. And she wasn't sharing. Cassie scooted the plate closer.

"I always thought of you," he said, his voice gentle, with a touch of regret.

Cassie choked on the second shrimp she'd shoved into her mouth. Did that line work for him? She waved her hands to show that she was okay, before he came around the table to pound on her back.

This man was going to pay. Was all his thinking about her before or after he broke her heart? Maybe it was after he told her he'd love her forever and then a few weeks later suggested they see other people. Perhaps it was the time he brought a "new special woman" home for Thanksgiving break.

"Actually, Dirk, I thought of you a lot, too."

His blue eyes sparkled. Hopeful. "Really?" he asked. "That's gr—"

"Yes, I don't care how old you get, how many times you fall in love, *find someone better*…you never forget the asshole who broke your heart first."

Dirk blanched, then took her hand. "Cass, I know, and I'm so—"

Every angry instinct in her body reacted. "Then something interesting happens. One day you stop crying and feeling sorry for yourself. You start to

question yourself. How could I have been so wrong? How could I have made such a mistake?"

He dropped her hand, then leaned back in his seat, giving her a scrutinizing look. "Like the title of your book," he said.

"Exactly." She smiled as she popped another shrimp into her mouth. "I searched and self-discovered and realized I hated you. And it was okay." She lifted her shoulders in a lighthearted shrug. "All those self-help books on the market talk about forgiveness, putting things in the past, blah blah blah."

His expression darkened. Good.

"I wanted to keep on hating you. So I gave myself permission to do it, and you know, I felt so much better afterwards. No high road involved." She gave a light chuckle, feeling better. Then she leaned forward as if she was telling him something in secret. "And apparently, a lot of other women in the world want to keep right on hating some jerk from their past, too, because the book has done very well."

"I'm really glad for you," he told her without a trace of irony in his voice. In fact, he was practically expressionless, which was faintly disappointing. She wanted him mad.

"I had dedicated my book to you, but my editor wouldn't let me use the word asshole. I couldn't think of anything better, so I dropped the whole idea." She paused, then her voice grew firm. "But the sentiment behind chapter nine is all about you."

"Well, I always wondered if you thought about me

once you left for Reno." His eyes met hers, and something a little bit like hunger simmered in their depths. "I only wanted you to be happy," he said without anger.

"Is that why you decided to post the tape on the Internet?" she asked him dryly.

"What tape?" he asked frowning.

She gave him a direct stare. Made a subtle head motion. "You know what tape. *The tape.* Of us."

Understanding appeared in his expression. "Oh, that tape. On the Internet. What are you talking about?"

Cassie eyed the seven or so shrimp she still had left. She hated letting the things go to waste. They were delicious.

She glanced at Dirk's confused face.

"I thought you might conveniently forget. I came prepared." Cassie reached for the envelope that had an image of him freeze-framed from the tape. It was a particularly embarrassing shot, with his face squeezed in a look of torture. Not the kind of photo you wanted your buddies to see. She'd also included a slip of paper with one of the Web addresses where she found excerpts of their tape.

She slid the package across the table to him. "This should refresh your memory."

He didn't reach for it. "You could have told me this on the phone."

"True, but over the telephone I couldn't tell you face-to-face what a despicable individual you are."

Cassie stood, pulling the strap of her purse over her shoulder. "Seeing that tape made me dream up a whole

new idea for a book. It will be all about the art of faking orgasm. And believe me when I say it *will* be dedicated to you. After all, you were the inspiration."

She turned on her delicate low heel and left.

DIRK TOSSED HIS NAPKIN on the table and watched as the one woman he'd never forgotten walk away from him. If anything, her ass had only gotten better with time. He reached across and grabbed one of her shrimp, then plopped it in his mouth.

The waiter came by with the bottle of wine. "Would you like to inspect the cork?"

Dirk glanced at the nearby couple celebrating. If everything had gone according to plan long ago, Dirk and Cassie would be toasting their fifth anniversary around this time. A little Cassie or little Dirk might have even made his or her appearance by now.

"Why don't you send it to that table over there," he said, indicating the joyful couple. "I'll take the bill."

Twenty minutes later, Dirk entered his house and stalked straight toward his computer, flinging his tie to the couch as he went. Although he suspected what was inside, he tore open the envelope while waiting for his software to load.

He glanced at the picture she'd supplied. Cassie had obviously printed the grainy image directly from the site. Unmistakably him. He winced at his agonized facial expression, clearly in the throes of passion. No one should ever see themselves like that.

He typed in the URL she'd given him, and the

images loaded almost instantly. Cassie's bedroom. He recognized the pink flowery sheets, the stuffed green bear he'd won for her at the fair and her Leonardo DiCaprio poster on the wall.

And there they were.

His fists balled up in anger. Angry and mad for so many things. Anger at letting Cassie go. Anger for her not giving him the chance he thought he needed to test the waters.

Hell, he'd only ever really dated one person in his life. Would it have hurt to evaluate their relationship by seeing other people? Cassie was his first date, his first kiss, his first…everything. He could also tack on to the end of that his *only*…everything. At twenty it had made perfect sense for them to "try out" other people to make sure they were meant to be together. He'd been an idiot to think she'd go along with the plan. He'd hurt her and she'd never forgiven him. Dirk learned too late how wrong he'd been, because nothing and no one ever compared to Cassie.

After she told him to get lost, and he realized what a colossal fool he'd been, he tried to win her back. He'd called, sent her flowers his college budget could barely afford and tried to see her on their college break schedules. But Cassie had distanced herself from him. A coolness settled around her, one he had no chance at melting. Finally Dirk realized things would never be how they once were. Cassie had moved on, and so had he.

Until she called him. He was a grown man, with a

wealth of experiences under his belt, but when he heard her voice, suddenly he was that lovesick boy again.

An image of his hands caressing her beautiful bare breasts flashed on the screen. How could he have let this happen? He was the one who was supposed to protect Cassie Coleman. A feminine moan emanated from the speakers on his computer. Cassie's feminine moan. Other people were seeing this, watching her. Something only meant for him. He'd failed her miserably and he could kick his own ass for letting it happen.

Another moan, and his body tightened. Anger became lust. It shouldn't be, but there it was. Everything about her had turned him on. Still did. When she walked in tonight with that blue dress, he was instantly tongue-tied and awkward, but knew with full-on certainty that *this* was what he wanted. Too bad he'd been too much of a fool not to hang on to the best thing that ever happened to him.

Dirk shut off the screen and headed for the kitchen. He needed a beer. Actually he wanted something harder. Getting drunk didn't sound half bad right now. But he needed to stay sharp in order to figure out how that tape got out of his possession. Tomorrow he'd start tracking it all down.

He still had one more thing to do tonight. After kicking off his shoes, he strode to the bookshelf. He opened up his well-worn copy of *How Could I Have Made Such a Mistake?—How To Have Mature, Adult Relationships While Still Hating the One Who Broke Your Heart.*

He was pretty sure he knew the topic of chapter nine, but he just wanted to confirm it in his mind. He flipped to the appropriate page.

There Always Has To Be One Person You Hate.

He closed the book with a smile. Yep, as he expected. Cassie hated him.

Sure, he probably deserved it, but that hadn't prevented him from harboring hope that she might want to rekindle things this evening. Who could blame him? After rebuffing him for so long, she finally called out of the blue.

He should be a nice guy, take care of the tape, then move on.

The book fell open on his lap, revealing the back cover with her picture. He traced the curve of her cheek, like he'd done many times before.

Dirk was done being the nice guy. He wanted Cassie Coleman, and he wouldn't get her by backing down. Yes, he was through playing nice. The nice guy never got the girl anyway.

He planned to get the girl. And keep her this time.

DANNI GOT COMFORTABLE on the blanket in front of the fire Eric had built. The blaze sent sparks and smoke into the air until they disappeared from sight. Out here, under the open expanse of the Nevada night sky, the stars were bright and many.

"One thing I never took for granted is the stars. I missed seeing them." She stared up at the moonless sky.

Eric settled beside her on the blanket, his big body

lending her warmth as the desert air cooled. He rolled on his back and looked at her. "I know what you mean," he said.

"A city boy, are you?" she asked.

He sat up abruptly. "Sometimes. How about a marshmallow? I brought some to roast."

Her mouth watered at the thought of warm, gooey marshmallows. "You certainly know how to get to a girl's heart," she said as he handed her a stick with a marshmallow on the tip.

Together they scooted closer to the fire. Their shoulders bumped, and she'd be lying if she didn't admit even that mediocre excuse for a caress felt good. Despite that naughty kiss in his office earlier today, Eric hadn't made a move to touch her.

There'd been plenty of opportunity for touching during their date. And for getting wet. Panning for gold turned out to be very physical work, and Eric approached it with a seriousness she'd come to recognize as his standard operating procedure. So when she "accidentally" splashed him with some water as she sifted the sand in her pan, it was really for his own good.

The fact that Eric "unintentionally" smeared cold wet mud on her calf only made Danni respect him more. They bumped elbows as they scraped out sand from the riverbed, and brushed feet in the cold water of the Truckee River. And not once did Eric make any move toward her. Really, he should have done something by now. Shouldn't he?

The fact was, she'd been pretty much off kilter and

confused with Eric since the moment he first asked for a dryer sheet.

Now they sat side by side on a blanket toasting their marshmallows and she hadn't gotten lips yet. She tried to ignore her feelings of confused frustration. Silence surrounded them, only the crackle of the popping fire breaking the stillness. And suddenly she realized she didn't need talking. Or kissing. Or anything. Right now was perfect.

Her marshmallow turned golden brown and she pulled her stick away from the fire. With careful fingers, she tugged the marshmallow off her stick and put it into her mouth. She closed her eyes with a slow moan. It tasted so good. "Delicious," she said as she licked her lips.

"Looked pretty good from here, too," he commented.

Their gazes locked, and even in the dark she could see the desire tinting his eyes. Perfect moment or not a minute ago, *this* was more like it. "I think this is the first time I've ever let a marshmallow get truly toasted. Usually I become so anxious I get it too close to the flame and it catches on fire."

He smiled as he stuck another marshmallow onto her stick. "I like slow and deliberate. Smooth and purposeful. That's how you get the satisfying outcome."

Okay, they weren't talking about toasting marshmallows. Her nipples hardened and her mouth went dry. Eric was giving her a preview of how he'd make love to her. Slow and deliberate. Smooth and purposeful. Satisfying outcome no doubt.

A shiver ran down her spine, and her skin flushed with need. She wanted Eric. Wanted him badly.

Strange because they were opposites. Eric was slow and deliberate, but she always thought of herself more like an arrow. Always moving. It didn't matter which direction her arrow pointed, just as long as it was moving. Now she didn't want to go so fast. She wanted to slow it down. Live the moment.

"I thought tonight might be dinner and a movie," she teased. "Typical date stuff."

Eric made a scoffing sound. "How can you get to know someone that way?"

His free hand reached for her chin, drawing her face closer. "And Danni, I do want to get to know you," he said. Then his mouth found hers in a gentle exploration.

Finally. She began to tighten her arms around his body. Wait, her stick. She opened her eyes to figure out where to dump it when she spotted his and laughed.

"Your marshmallow is on fire," she told him.

Eric gave her a crooked smile then gave his stick and hers a toss, sending them both into the fire.

He pulled her against his chest that let her know this would be no gentle exploration. That's exactly what *she* wanted. Danni met him lip for lip in a kiss filled with hunger and desire.

7

"HE WALKED ME TO THE DOOR, gave me a kiss good-night, and he left," Danni told Cassie later that night, as she twisted the phone cord between her fingers. A heated rush ran along her skin as she remembered that amazing kiss.

"Hmm, he didn't even try to maneuver himself inside? Did you at least invite him in?"

Danni's shoulders slumped. "No and yes. He declined. I don't get it. We had a great date. I couldn't have organized something as romantic without a lot of recon. And when he kissed me—"

"Wait. You've skipped something. I thought it was a quick kiss good-night. A peck, but this sounds different."

It certainly felt a lot different than a chaste brush of his lips. A warmth turned her muscles all soft. Despite her best efforts not to turn into a sap, Danni knew she was smiling. "No, it was earlier. As we were roasting marshmallows. His caught on fire and suddenly we were kissing."

"You understand I'm working really hard not to make a sarcastic comment about roasting marshmallows."

Danni laughed. "Yes, and I appreciate the effort. I really do." She blew out her breath, making her bangs

ruffle. "Man, when did you become the cynic? Usually I reserve that spot."

"Friend role reversal. It's common in long-term female relationship bonds. So, you got lips. How was it?"

Danni sucked in a breath, her skin was achy with the erotic memory of Eric's arms around her. His big, hard body pressed tight against hers. "Amazing," she said, hating herself for giving into a dreamy sigh. "It was strange. We just kissed and kissed and kissed."

"Ahhh, you're bringing back young dating memories," Cassie said, her tone wistful. "That's called macking. I love dates like those. I used to do that with Dirk on my back porch. He'd leave and all I could think of was when we'd kiss again." She made a little growling sound. "Now those kisses are immortalized on the Internet."

That's exactly how Eric had left her. Thinking only of him. And when she'd get the opportunity for more macking. And she'd felt off balance ever since.

Some of the glow shifted downward and faded. Was that Eric's angle? Had he left her wanting more tonight, so she'd be clamoring for him later?

Now who was being the cynic? Danni shook her head. Smooth and purposeful. That's how Eric lived his life. That would be the way he dealt with relationships. She'd have a lot of fun trying to break him out of his staid ways. And soon. She wanted him. In spite of how off balance he made her feel.

"Speaking of Dirk. How did it go tonight?" Danni asked, ready to shift the conversation.

There was a long, telling pause before Cassie

answered. "Let's say I won't be needing those acting skills."

Danni laughed. "So, no spark still there?"

Silence was her only answer. Danni sat up a tad straighter, her ears perked a little. Was this avoidance or was her friend thinking?

"Cassie?" she prompted.

"No. None. No spark at all," her friend rushed to tell her.

Liar. But that was okay. She'd let her friend work it out on her own. "So, had he really let himself go? How bad did he look?" Danni asked, trying to keep the smile out of her voice.

"Unfortunately he didn't look bad at all," Cassie said with a grumble. "Don't worry. I did what I had to do. I told him off. I left him with a huge bill, too," she said chuckling.

Danni gave her friend a mental high five. "Excellent. So you're driving back tomorrow?"

"Absolutely. First thing. I'll call you when I get back."

THEY SAID THEIR goodbyes, and Cassie replaced the receiver on the pink phone in her old bedroom. Choosing that pink phone seemed a million years ago. Her gaze scanned the bedroom of her teenage years. Mom hadn't done much to it except take down her old posters.

Cassie tossed her blue dress over a chair and pulled on a UNLV T-shirt and some sweatpants. She slumped on the mattress and slipped off her watch to set it on the table next to her bed. That table had once basically

been an homage to her relationship with Dirk. Pictures of him. Pictures of them together. But after that second year at college, she'd tossed every last one of the photos into a shoe box and shoved it under the bed. She still remembered the hurt and pain she felt when she first saw him with another girl.

Cassie sank to her knees and yanked the box out from under the bed frame. Still there.

As a licensed counselor with years of training and experience, she knew removing the photos but not destroying them was her way of keeping hope alive that her relationship with Dirk would one day repair itself.

As a grown woman, she knew it was time to pitch them all into the trash. Maybe even set them on fire. Now that was a great idea. In her book she'd even given a few safety tips on having a cleansing fire ritual with relationship memorabilia. Her mom wouldn't be back from her Red Hat meeting for several more hours, so she'd have plenty of time to set Dirk's face aflame without having to offer any explanations.

This felt right.

Grabbing a bottle of wine from the fridge, and a metal coffee can from the garage, she headed for the backyard. Cassie yanked the photos from the frames and dumped them into the can. With the water hose on standby, she struck a match and set everything aflame.

The heat of the blaze warmed her cheeks and her spirits.

In her book she'd suggested inviting friends to watch the fire or even playing a favorite "together"

song as the flames caught. But she liked the simplicity of tonight, with only the crickets and the crackle and pop of the fire to keep her company. She smiled as she took a swig from the wine bottle.

The smell of sulfur from the match and burning paper filled the air. Bits of ash floated into the night sky like black snow in reverse. Deep breath in. Deep breath out. She totally embraced the calm. Not a regret in sight.

The creak of her mother's trellis alerted Cassie that she was no longer alone. Normally the sounds of someone climbing over the fence would have alarmed her, but some sixth sense told her the person now destroying her mother's roses was Dirk and not some intruder. The groan of straining wood ended with a sudden snap from the aged fence and the sound of a large body hitting the ground.

"Damn it," said the owner of the large body.

Yes, definitely Dirk.

The leaping flames died down, and with a few squirts of the hose, the fire sizzled and spurted to its end. She watched as the last orange ember turned to gray ash. How many times had Dirk snuck over that fence? Too many times to count.

This blew. Here she was erasing his memories, and he comes barreling over her fence like he had when they were fifteen and wanted to be alone together.

After brushing off her hands, she turned to face him. He leaned against the siding, trying to look casual and unassuming, and not at all like a man who'd just fallen on his ass.

"I'm a lot better now," he told her, that rich voice of his caressing her in the dark.

Her back stiffened and she heard the blood pound in her ears. "I doubt it," she told him after she realized he was talking about his technique on the sex tape and not some weird psychic reaction to her setting his pictures ablaze. Or his backside.

Dirk laughed. Sexy and low and in a way she didn't remember. All man and full of confidence now. Not the green fumbling teenager in the dark. Her breath grew shallow.

"It's something I'd prove."

And despite it all, she felt a tingle of awareness. Maybe it was the recent nostalgia. Maybe it was because the back porch light only gave the hints and shadows of his rugged face, but Cassie knew, on some elemental level, that sex with Dirk in the present would be amazing. It hadn't been all that bad years ago, bordering more on emotion than sensation. But now it would be both.

"I called a while ago. What were you doing? Were you thinking of me?" he asked, his voice husky, as if he were thinking of her naked.

She rolled her eyes. Dirk never used to ask those kinds of questions. "Actually, I was burning your effigy in my backyard."

"Really?" he asked, sounding worried.

Good. "Oh, did I say that out loud? Because I meant to say that out loud."

"I bet you look hot. What are you wearing? I can barely see you."

Cassie gasped at his gall. Secretly intrigued and hating herself for it. *Chapter Nine.*

Someone to hate.

Focus. It was all blinking loud and clear. "A housecoat. Something my grandma gave me. Used."

Yet somehow his outrageous comments didn't make her angry. No, they excited her. Thrilled her. Now was not the time for this. She felt more vulnerable somehow, here at night, surrounded by dozens of memories of them together in her backyard. Playing in the sprinkler as children. Kissing under the tree.

"I bet you look fantastic. I can't describe the agony I was in when I imagined you asleep in your bedroom. Under the covers. I'd wake up hard. I've never wanted anyone like I want you."

Her breath hitched, and it became harder to breathe. *I want you.* Present tense. Cassie was a person who noticed grammar. Dirk knew that. He pushed himself off the side of her house, and walked toward her.

"You need to leave," she told him.

"Have dinner with me tomorrow night," he said. It wasn't an invitation…more like an encouragement. *Have dinner with me. Let me do amazing stuff to your body.* Her breasts grew heavy. She wouldn't let herself imagine what that stuff would be.

Let me humiliate you in front of the world.

"No, thank you," she replied. "I'm leaving tomorrow morning anyway."

He nodded toward the bottle she'd left on the picnic table. "Then share your wine with me now."

"If there's to be any drinking together, you'd be buying. And I don't drink cheap wine."

"I think I can manage your preferences on my budget," he said. A small laugh from him told her he knew she'd rung up the dinner bill on purpose and that he didn't care.

"Besides," he continued, "I never got to finish my end of the conversation tonight. You owe me that."

She righted herself. So did her breathing. "I don't owe you a damn thing."

"Then you owe it to yourself. Don't you want to know what I have to say?"

She hesitated. *Say no. Say no. Say no.* But what did he want to say? Curiosity did a lot more than kill the cat. Danni always said curiosity was a bad thing. Now she understood why.

An intensity surrounded him, as if he was ready to do battle. The question was why. Her thoughts grabbed on to the tips in Chapter Two. *Confront Up Front.*

"What do you want?" she asked, not bothering to hide her confusion. He was her Chapter Nine. Her one person to hate. She was good with that. It worked.

More important, she didn't want to change that, but it seemed like Dirk had other ideas.

He reached for her hand, twining his fingers between hers. So familiar. "I want to spend time with you. Talk. Get to know you again," he said, his gaze direct. His voice strong and not sounding a bit strange in spite of the romantic things he was saying. Dirk was not a romantic.

"No," she said, flat, emotionless.

In spite of her refusal, she could see his smile in the night. "Why not?" he asked, appearing as if he liked the idea of the challenge.

She thrust his hand away. "Hmm, let's see. You let me down. You broke my heart. The most intimate moments I could ever spend with you are now a personal sex education class for any fourteen-year-old boy with a low-speed modem. Half those sites aren't even password protected."

"It's not that bad," he said, his voice taking on a re-assuring tone, as if he wanted to comfort her.

Cassie sucked in a breath. "Maybe not to you. You're the stud on Ibangedherdotcom."

Dirk reached for her elbow, his thumb gently caressing her skin. "What I said earlier is true. I never stopped thinking of you."

She made a scoffing noise.

"I was an idiot. I made the biggest mistake of my life when I let you go. I want to fix that mistake now. I'll start by finding out who took our tape. It was stolen, Cassie. I didn't do it. I want you to know that. I would never do anything to hurt you."

He seemed sincere. And the words…he was saying every single word in exactly the way her twenty-year-old self would have wanted to hear them.

Her twenty-nine-year-old self wanted to grab the bottle of wine she wouldn't share and dump it over his head. "Not interested."

His lips turned sultry, his gaze heated. "It's still

there between us, Cassie. The spark. The hunger. I could see it in your eyes tonight. Feel it in the tenseness of your body right now. You want me. I damn well know I want you."

A shaft of awareness splintered through her chest, and warmth rushed between her legs. The idea of this big, sexy man still wanting her after all these years made her body yearn for his touch. She forced herself to harden her response. Cut off the desire.

"Ahh, but, Dirk, I am not a jerk. And I don't want you."

"Not true," he challenged. His thumb continued to caress the sensitive skin of her wrist.

Goose bumps formed on her arm. She knew Dirk felt them—she *felt* the excitement in him.

"Oh, my body may want you, but to borrow a tip from my third chapter—second helpings are merely cold servings left over from the first time. There's a reason the entrée was returned to the kitchen."

He dropped her hand, but didn't seem at all fazed by her rejection. "That was a chapter I just couldn't get into."

8

ERIC STUDIED THE PICTURE he'd printed of Danni from the casino's database. The openness and honesty of her now didn't mesh with the sullen-faced girl in the photo. But then, no one looked good in a mug shot.

He slipped her picture into a file folder and pushed the whole thing away to a corner of his desk. For some reason he didn't want to think of her as a broken, forgotten teen trying to find her place in a world that didn't want her, with a father who couldn't stay out of jail. A person who spent her high school years behind bars. Albeit deservedly so.

He much preferred Danni as she had been last night. Smart and funny and a woman he wanted to know better. A woman he'd like to help stay on her current path of legitimacy. Which made no sense at all.

People were supposed to trust *him*. Yet he found himself wanting to trust *her*. He wasn't supposed to want things from them either. Not their breath on his heated skin. Not the joy they made him feel.

He slammed a drawer shut. Last night wasn't right. Last night felt like a serious date. He had a job to do,

and dating, at least that kind of dating, wasn't part of it. Keeping it casual was the key.

And printing off her picture was far from casual. He shoved her folder into a nearby cabinet. Couldn't have Danni finding that.

His cell phone rang. Eric didn't have to glance at the caller ID to know it was his supervisor needing another progress report. Now was not a good time. Danni was meeting him here for lunch, and he had things to set up.

For the first time he felt frustration with his career. When he'd taken this job, the casino had been nothing but an opportunity. A chance to move up the ladder. He never dreamed he'd find something here he might want to hold on to after it was all over.

SHE WOULD NOT BE A SAP. *She would not be a sap.* Danni said this to herself over and over again as she walked through the casino toward Eric's office.

Her father would say Eric had her on the run. After all, she was doing the legwork and coming to him, meeting him on *his* turf. But this was a healthy, adult relationship. Her first. And things like legwork and power balances didn't figure in healthy adult relationships. Of that she was mildly confident.

Eric's door was open. Her heart rate increased and her palms grew moist. This was probably a typical teenager's response to seeing a guy who you really really liked, and macked with the night before.

Except she was a grown woman. Still, despite the

fact that she missed out on all the typical coming of age angst, she planned to explore every emotion and sensation, and enjoy it the way a woman should.

Danni popped her head around the doorframe. His office was empty. She tamped down her small sense of disappointment. What should she do? Hang around outside his door? Go inside and have a seat? She had absolutely no social skills where this kind of situation was concerned.

And yes, she'd quash that first instinct that an empty office was a ripe opportunity. Opportunity to rifle through all his things. No. She'd sit down in one of the guest chairs, cross her legs at the ankles and demurely place her hands in her lap. Not a problem. She could even consider this moment as a moment of quiet from her job and her studies, and meditate or something. For that matter, she could embrace the calm.

Except about twenty seconds into her imposed tranquility, her gaze fell upon the file on Eric's desk. The one marked Security. And its twin marked Banned.

Out it came. The Flynn Family Curiosity. An amateur might think that snooping and reconnaissance were identical. Semantically, probably very similar…but in application. One got you thrown into jail, and the other kept you out.

Asking yourself questions like, "What would one small peek hurt?" or "Who would know?" would also get you thrown out of your new hot and utterly normal boyfriend's office.

So she could wait. Patiently, too. Her gaze moved

around the room. He still didn't have anything in his office. Maybe she could change that. She felt a grin on her face. She sure liked the way that sounded.

Seven minutes and thirty-seven seconds later, Eric strolled into the room. The tense expression left his face when he saw her.

She loved knowing her presence alone could make him feel better. Now that was a whole lot better than embracing the calm.

"I'm sorry, I got stuck on the floor. Were you waiting long?" he asked.

"No." *Lie.*

At her words, Eric flashed her a smile that sent shivers all over her body and straight through to her toes. She could have waited forever for that smile. "The hotel has opened a new restaurant. You up for Chinese?"

"Absolutely."

Should she mention the files on his desk? Perhaps remind him he shouldn't leave important items like that lying around? Then he reached around her and locked the door, pulling it shut after them.

"Do you always lock your door?"

Eric nodded. "Always."

"But it was wide open when I arrived."

"I knew you'd be coming."

She smiled, growing as warm and tingly as if he'd kissed her. Eric trusted her. And the feeling was wonderful. Good call on not lifting up the file folder for a quick peek.

"The restaurant is off the casino floor," he said,

leading the way. After they ordered, they were left alone to talk. It occurred to her that since Eric had taken over the date planning, he'd created a lot of chances to talk.

"Tell me about the first time you cheated someone."

Her back stiffened. He hadn't brought this up since her confession. She would have preferred miniature golf to this.

"It's okay," he urged.

Danni gave Eric a hard, scrutinizing look. Searching for any sign of judgment or distaste. But she found only curiosity in his eyes. This is what people did, right? They got to know one another. That had to include everything.

"In the fifth grade a girl down the street tricked me into giving her my favorite Barbie. By the end of the week, I got it back plus her Barbie Corvette."

Eric laughed. "How'd you do that?"

Danni shrugged. "I don't remember anymore. Probably a combination of misdirection and flattery. Dad said I had the perfect hustle. Mom said I should be ashamed of myself. It was the only time I ever saw my parents argue. Dad was a con man before he married her, but gave up the game for her. She required it."

"How did your mom die?"

Danni sipped her iced tea. "Accident. Dad took off for a while after that, and I went to live with my grandparents. It was my last real home, I missed her so much. This sounds so—" Danni's words broke off. She sat surprised at the tightness in her throat. So many years had passed, and she'd talked about her mother

dozens of times in counseling sessions during her incarceration, and then later with Cassie. Danni hadn't felt teary in a long while. So why now?

Eric kept silent, waiting patiently.

Danni cleared her throat. "Sometimes when I was in a store and there'd be a girl about my age with her mom, I'd kind of sidle up to them, and stand close and pretend. For just a moment, I'd imagine the woman was my mother. Smell her perfume. Try to memorize what she was wearing."

Danni lifted her chin and gave him a wink. "About nine months later, Dad dropped in, picked me up and brought me to Vegas, and gave me an education. Flynn Family style."

"He taught you to steal," he said matter-of-factly.

She lifted a finger. "He taught me the art of the con," she said in an impression of her father's real voice.

"Is there a difference?" he asked, his expression turning sour.

"Not really, but in his mind there is. You see, Dad came from a long line of conning Flynns. They developed rules over the years. I'm sure it was to mask the guilt of taking someone else's property."

Danni's and Eric's food arrived, and Danni took a bite of her beef and broccoli. "Mmm, this is good. Excellent choice of restaurant. Yours looks good, too."

"You want a bite?" he asked. He swirled some of the Asian noodle dish on his fork, then tipped it toward her. Danni leaned forward, taking the fork into her mouth slowly.

Danni's eyes never left his as her lips closed over the delicious bite he offered. Her teeth snagged the end of the bite, and she pulled it into her mouth. She closed her eyes on a sigh.

Eric swallowed. "That looked really good," he said. His voice was husky, letting her know his mind wasn't all on food.

"See how easy it is?"

"To what?" he asked.

"I just conned you out of a bite of your food."

He raised an eyebrow. "Maybe I wanted to give it to you."

"And there's Flynn Con Rule Number One. Find something that people don't mind losing."

"People don't want their money taken."

"True. But sometimes they don't mind if you leave them with a good feeling. Find the need they have inside, appeal to it. That's where the art comes in."

"So, a moment ago, when your mouth closed around that fork but your eyes made me think about your lips on my body, was that a con?"

She knew she was blushing. "I'm out of the hustle business. That was all me."

Eric's gaze turned heated. "That's good to know." After a few minutes, he asked, "You think you can con me?"

"It would be hard, you're looking for it now. I'd need to spend a lot of time with you, do a lot of research to find out your weaknesses."

"Feel free to do all the research you need to on

my body," he offered, sliding the back of his hand down her arm.

"Very generous," she said with a laugh.

"So how's your life changed since you left juvie?"

"Well, I'll never wear orange again for as long as I live." She laughed even though it was true. Then she became more contemplative. "You know, I never thought I'd tell anyone but Cassie about my past." Everything with Eric felt so easy.

He looked genuinely surprised, and maybe a tad uncomfortable. For a moment, Danni wondered if she'd shared a little too much.

"You haven't told anyone, not even one of those old musician boyfriends?" he asked.

"You'd think, but no. Maybe it would have made me look cooler in their eyes. Criminal girlfriend," she said wryly. Then she took a deep breath, ready to lay all her cards on the table. "It's probably because deep down I didn't trust them enough."

Eric's movement stilled, his direct gaze met hers. "Do you trust me, Danni?"

A smile tugged at her lips. "Yes."

The expression on his face didn't change. "Don't even have to think about it?"

She shook her head. "No, I don't even have to think about it."

His hand reached across the table for hers, stilling her restless fingers. "I want you to know I'll always take care of your interests."

She smiled despite the odd phrasing. Maybe that's

how people in the corporate world would say, "Come on, baby, I don't need to wear one of those things."

"So, do you trust me?" she asked, really needing to know. Afraid of the answer. Who'd trust her?

He blinked at her, his gaze slid away, then he met her eyes full force with those sexy brown eyes of his. "Yes," he admitted.

Danni laughed. "Don't sound so surprised."

"I guess I hadn't thought of it until this moment."

Eric signaled for the bill, and she placed her fingers on his hand. "I should get this. You've paid for the last few meals."

"I'm using my free comps," he told her in a conspiratorial whisper.

"You see, I'm having a bad influence on you already."

"I think I kind of like it."

A few minutes later, they walked hand in hand through the casino. She noted that there were lots of new games since her last extended stint inside a casino, not including the other day. But she didn't get to gawk for long since Eric had her buzzing across the floor at a quick pace.

"Wait," she said, and he halted beside her. "Casually look at the guy in the blue polo shirt."

Danni watched as Eric's gaze slid toward the man she indicated. "What's wrong with him?" he asked.

"He's cheating."

Eric's body instantly turned rigid, all attention focused on the man. Danni tugged on his hand. "Come on, you'll warn him."

Eric reluctantly followed beside her. "What was he doing?"

"He was card-holing. Did you see the woman with the glasses standing behind the dealer? She was trying to spot the dealer's hole card. If she spotted it, she'd signal to the man in blue and he'd make his bets."

"I take it you don't approve?"

Obviously he'd heard the disgust in her voice. "Advantage gamblers are the worst. I mean, where's the sport in that? You don't take someone's money without at least giving them something in return. A good story at least."

He stopped, his hand turning her to face him. "Do you really believe that?" Eric's expression was serious. "All this talk, all this hype about conning and taking, is that really behind you?"

A tense energy seemed to surround his body. As if a lot was riding on her answer.

Danni nodded her head to indicate yes. "Absolutely. I went to jail for it. And believe me when I tell you, jail is no place I ever want to go back to."

Eric traced the curve of her cheek tenderly. The tension was gone, replaced now by a look so heated her nerve endings felt scorched. "I can't tell you how relieved I am to hear that," he said against her lips.

His kiss did scorch her. And she wanted to be burned all over her body.

9

AFTER THAT KISS in the hallway, Eric quickly led her to the elevators. Her legs were weak and her stomach muscles tightened in need.

"Come upstairs," he said. He wasn't asking. He was only voicing what they both wanted.

Danni nodded, her heart pounding and nipples hardening in anticipation. Soon he'd be touching her. Kissing her.

They managed to keep their hands off each other until the elevator door closed, then Danni slammed his shoulders against the wall. He reached for her hips, deliciously crushing her body to his rock-solid chest. The hard ridge of his erection rubbed between her legs, sending a shaft of wet warmth through her core.

She kissed him hard. Long. And with passion. Her tongue traced the lips she'd thought about during lunch. Eric clutched her upper arms, and his breathing grew harsh. She smiled against his mouth. Her controlled corporate man had lost his smooth, methodical moves from the night before. Now Eric was raw and instinctive as he stroked and palmed her breasts through her blouse.

Danni loved it. Reveled in knowing her body, her mouth, *she* caused this controlled man to sink to primal need. The ding of the elevator alerted them to Eric's floor. She was almost reluctant to pull away.

The door opened with a whoosh, and a puff of air hit her heated skin. With his hand at the small of her back, Eric guided her to his room. She'd never walked so fast to get someplace, even when she was late for class. They reached his room and Eric smashed the keycard into the slot and the door unlocked.

Once inside, her purse hit the floor, and he kicked the door shut. Eric leaned against it and pulled her to his big strong body, mirroring their positions in the elevator. His hands sank into her hair, bringing her mouth closer, harder to his.

"I want you naked." They were his rough words, but she felt the same way.

His fingers trailed up her back, a touch like fire against her skin. She sucked in a breath as he teased and tormented each vertebra and she twisted and ground her hips against him in pleasure.

"So sexy," he breathed.

Eric found the loop of fabric holding the top of her camisole in place. With a few deft turns of his fingers the material fell to her waist and his hands caressed her shoulders, lifting her gently away.

"I want to look at you," he said, his voice tight with tension.

Her nipples hardened even more before his gaze, increasing her pleasure.

For a moment, he simply stared at her near naked body. She felt like the sexiest woman alive.

"You're so beautiful and exciting. I wasn't expecting that," he told her on a husky groan.

"What were you expecting?" she asked.

Eric's eyes widened for a moment, then he lowered his mouth to first one rose-tipped breast, and the other. She gasped in red-hot need at the rasping of his tongue. All her thoughts and questions disappeared and she only felt. Felt his heated breath against the sensitive skin of her nape. Thrilled in the delicious sensation of his warm, wet mouth.

She'd have preferred to have been the seducer, the one setting the pace. Then she'd have the control.

Danni moaned as he swirled her nipple with his tongue.

But sometimes sacrifices must be made.

Eric grabbed her skirt, bunching it higher along her thigh. Her skin tingled as he ran his fingers along her bare legs.

"You're so soft."

"Mmm," she moaned, and lifted one leg to bring her most responsive areas into direct contact with his erection. She rubbed herself against him, sending sparks of delicious intensity crashing through her.

"Do that again," he urged. His voice was a seductive invitation. His hands cupped her backside, dragging her higher against his body, harder against the long length of his cock.

She rubbed her body up and down the ridge of his penis, seeking the best spot. They were all good.

His tongue slid along the sensitive area above her collarbone, and she bucked against him. "Right there," he said, his voice full with need.

Her movements became more frantic. Eric's hands wound around her hips, guiding her frenzied motion. She moaned, rubbing herself harder. Faster. Every muscle contracted. Danni squeezed her eyes tight, clutched his shoulders. She was so close. So close.

He thrust his hips against hers.

"Oh, my— I'm c—" She couldn't speak. Her words broke off as one amazing sensation overtook another. Every muscle of her back stiffened and the sound of her gasping cry echoed throughout the small entrance-way of his hotel suite. She couldn't breathe. Couldn't open her eyes. How her heart managed to beat she'd never know.

Corporate was so hiding something good.

She should be a wreck. She should be nothing but a lump, but that orgasm only left her energized. Her body ached to do that again. This time with them both naked between the sheets. Or against the wall. Only the naked part mattered.

She lifted her head, already missing the heated clean scent of his neck. Her eyes drifted open to see the strain around his lips. The tightness of his shoulders. Sweat beaded along his forehead.

Her heartbeat slowed to a mere race and her heavy panting subsided. The air unit kicked on. They must

have generated some incredible heat. An embarrassed blush rose in her cheeks. She'd barely let the man pass the threshold before she romped on him.

Their eyes met in the fading daylight coming from the bedroom window. It was too dark to make out what lay in his beautiful brown depths, but the force of his passion bombarded her.

She worked up a weak smile. "I can't believe that. I've never…I mean, I don't even have my clothes off. And you…you didn't even get to enjoy anything."

His deep laugh turned into a low, pained groan. Every muscle in his neck strained. His skin hot to the touch.

"Believe me, I enjoyed it. But I'm in a bad way," he told her.

Every nerve ending in her body let out one big *hmm*. *She'd* gotten him in that bad way. Her embarrassment faded. Obviously seeing her orgasm, relish in her own pleasure made him want her. He'd be an amazing lover. Danni couldn't wait to find out.

She grabbed his hand as Eric pushed himself from the wall. "I can take care of that," she offered, her gaze shifted downward to openly admire his body.

She'd never been in such a large suite before, but had no urge to explore the space. Danni found his bedroom off a small sitting area. The king bed was topped with a soft comforter, which she quickly shoved away. She turned and saw Eric lift his shirt.

"Wait," she said. "Let me."

The material fell from his hands, as she stalked toward him. She had no plans to delicately recline

against the headboard and watch the silhouette of her future lover remove his clothes. She wanted him naked. And she wanted to get him that way.

She grabbed for the hem of his polo shirt, then lifted it slowly up his body, her fingers trailing up the warmth of his skin. Her fingers ached to touch the newly revealed hard muscles of his chest and to trace that tantalizing line of crinkly hair down the tautness of his flat stomach. First, she had to finish stripping him, leaving him in only his underwear.

That is if he wore underwear.

Danni's whole body shivered as that image flooded her mind. Her fingers quickly found the button and zip of his pants, and she swiftly shoved them down his solid thighs.

Boxer briefs. Sexy as hell.

Danni fought a war between disappointment of him not being completely naked, and the thrill of knowing she'd be seeing him in the buff after tearing off that scrap of material. With her teeth.

She scooted onto the bed, bringing him down with her. The bed dipped invitingly under his weight. She had no hint of "first time" nerves.

"I want you so bad. Hearing you come like that, it was so damn erotic," he whispered, his breath teasing her skin. He reached for her ankles, fingering the gold chain adorning the smooth skin above her left foot. His fingers traced the line of her calf, the sensitive skin behind her knee, up her thighs. Her body tensed in anticipation. "I'm going to make you come and come again."

Then his hand moved down.

Danni sucked in a breath, holding it as he shifted to her right leg. With a firm push, he positioned her knees on either side of his hips and kneeled between her legs. He followed the path his fingers took again, but this time with his palms. His touch became more forceful, deepening her excitement. He didn't stop at the barrier of her bunched up skirt. Her stomach muscles clenched as the calloused skin of his hands moved along her belly and up her rib cage.

Touch my breasts. Hold them. Suck them.

She arched toward him, her nipples tightening in expectation.

A moan tore from her throat as he molded her breasts the way she wanted him to. Sweeter and more delicious than earlier. Her knees clamped around him.

"Hey, who put you in charge?" she asked.

He angled her face toward him. "I've always been in charge," he said against her lips.

She expected another firm, hard kiss. Instead, he tongued the outer ridge of her lips. He gently tugged her bottom lip into his mouth.

He rolled and stretched beside her. Danni sunk her hands into the hair at the back of his neck, urging, drawing him nearer to turn his carnal caress into a real kiss.

But he was too quick for her, his dark head sinking to her side. "I want to taste your skin," he growled against her ear.

Danni breathed deep, her body nearly writhing. The

tip of his tongue touched the curve of her ear in one luscious stroke.

"Take me into your body, Danni. Take me like this," he told her, his voice urgent.

Describing how he wanted her was almost as yummy as she knew the real thing would be. She reached for his hips. "Yes. Now."

"Wait," he whispered. His hands stilled hers.

He lowered his head to kiss the hollow of her neck. With a gentle squeeze, he released her hands and trailed his own down her body. Her nipples tightened against the light touch of his fingers. The fine hairs along her skin tingling as he stopped between her legs, his fingers searching between the folds of the material.

After one long, agonizing moment, he cupped her. His fingers teased and stroked her slick heat. Deep pleasurable agony pierced her as his thumb found her clit. A shot of desire raced to her core.

She wanted him *now*.

A feeling of delicious rightness flowed through her body. Yes. The hardness of him pressed into her thigh. Everything felt so, so right.

Eric groaned as he gripped the edge of her skirt and tugged. She was lying on it, and the voluminous folds grew awkward.

"Just leave it. Rip it, I don't care."

Eric grabbed the thin material of her panties and tore the material apart in such a way that the force didn't hurt her. He tossed the material to the floor.

The cool air touched her hot, bare skin, and she dug her toes into the softness of the mattress.

She wanted to touch him. She needed to taste him, too. Danni shifted upward and kissed his chest, trailing her fingers down his stomach. His skin twitched as her fingers found the band of his boxer briefs.

To hell with the slowness of taking them off with her teeth. She wanted them off now. Her fingers trembled slightly as she pulled them down. In the past, she'd hidden her boldness, what she liked in bed. Something about his open need of her bolstered her confidence. She wanted him to know how much he affected her. How much she wanted him. Period. Her hand found his erection and she encircled him, eliciting a broken moan.

Her lips soon followed her fingers. At the base of him, she licked her lips then ran her tongue up his smooth hard length. Eric shuddered.

"Do you want me to stop?" she asked, her voice teasing. She knew he didn't want her to pause even a mini-second.

"No, no."

She tormented the tip of him with her tongue, then fully took him in her mouth. Above her, he groaned and his hips jumped. His fingers twined through her hair. She loved what she did to him, never realizing the kind of power her touch had over him.

With a jerk, he cupped his hands under her arms and pulled her up to him. He rolled her onto her back. The heat in his eyes told her he had big plans for her. Naughty plans.

He kissed his way down her body, the tip of his nose tickling her skin. She arched even before his tongue found her. She gasped at the first gentle swipe, then he tasted her in one long glorious stroke after another.

"Now, Eric, now."

"I need something to protect you," he said.

"Nothing in the nightstand?" she asked, a wave of frustration pummeling her body.

"There was a sex toy convention at the hotel a few days ago. They were practically throwing the condoms around. I left them on the table in the front room."

"More comps?" Now, something for nothing was something her con artist soul could appreciate.

She flipped on the bedside light so he could see where he was going. Watching his sweet ass as he walked away was something she could appreciate, too. Soon she'd be grabbing those muscular cheeks of his as he thrust into her. A new rush of warmth heated between her legs.

A moment later, he returned to the bedroom. Eric was amazing to look at from the molded strength of his thighs, the muscled flatness of his stomach to those brown eyes of his, almost black with sexual tension. Her eyes were drawn to his penis. Still thick and erect. She wouldn't be turning off the light soon.

Eric held up a package. "This one warms up with friction. Inside and out." He tore off the corner of the package with his teeth, then sheathed himself.

He stretched beside her on the bed, nudging her legs apart with his knee. The wide tip of him teased where she ached to welcome him. Frustration gnawed

at her. She rotated her hips, his penis rubbing, making her blood heat. He entered her in one long, controlled thrust, filling her and making her tremble.

He groaned when he finally rested totally within her, and her eyes drifted shut.

"Open your eyes," he said in a gruff voice, his words stilted and spoke of his need.

With difficulty she happily blinked open her eyes. The lamplight fell across his face. Their gazes met. Fire blazed from his brown depths. When he had her full attention, he pulled almost all the way out, her body protesting every millimeter's withdrawal. Then he pushed forward again.

She raised her chin, gripping his shoulders tightly.

"Do you feel that?"

"I'm feeling everything."

He chuckled low in his throat. "No, the condom. Do you feel the heat?"

She shook her head.

"Wait," he said, the assurance in his voice making all kinds of sexy noncorporate-type promises. He withdrew from her once more.

She bit her lip as he sank back again. Ahhh. A strange stirring heat fired her from the inside. She tingled wherever he stroked. "That's amazing."

He thrust inside her again and again. His body continued with the maddening rhythm until they were both gasping.

He stopped suddenly, and every hormone in her body screamed. "This isn't right," he said.

Danni clamored for release. "Feels right to me."

He drew from her body, then he wrapped her in those big arms of his. "I want it like it was in the hall," he ordered.

Her senses became even more in tune to him as he lifted her from the bed and put her back against the closest wall, settling her legs around his waist. He entered her in one incredible thrust. The heat from him scorched her. She met him, moved against him as she had in the entryway.

A powerful rush of satisfaction washed over her and cascaded through her body. She clutched him within her. Hard. Eric must have been waiting for that second orgasm of hers because he lost his careful strokes. Moving above her, within her, until all the powerful muscles of his back stiffened, he all but shouted her name. A fulfillment like nothing she'd ever felt before took her over.

Her whole body felt languid and sated. She collapsed against his chest, smiling into his neck. After a few moments, Danni lowered her legs, taking her weight off Eric. When her feet found the soft carpet of the floor, she looked up into his eyes.

The muscles along his chest and neck were still tense, but when he opened his eyes he visibly relaxed. He gave her a slow sexy smile that had her immediately thinking of round two.

"Teach me how to count cards, Danni," he said. And she wouldn't have been more surprised if he'd asked her to knock over a convenience store.

10

"WHAT, I DON'T GET room service first?" Danni asked once they were in the bed and under the covers. Eric didn't laugh. She shifted onto her elbows to get a better look into his eyes. "You're serious. Why do you want to know?"

His fingers drew lazy patterns against her hip. "When you were pointing out that gambler downstairs, the thought occurred to me that maybe you could show me a few things."

"You always think business after you come?"

Eric's hand tightened on her hip, drawing her closer to his body. "I thought it could be something we'd do together. I have a lot of things in mind for us to do together," he told her, evoking all kinds of wicked thoughts in her mind.

"So, am I going to be the Bonnie to your Elliot Ness?"

"I think we work pretty great as a team," he said as his fingers moved along her bare thigh.

And she had the aftershocks to prove it.

Eric's face grew more serious. "Blackjack is the only beatable game in the casino. If I want to defeat

someone who is trying to win by counting cards, then I need to learn how to do it."

"Makes a lot of sense." She gave him a dubious glance. "Am I just expected to hand over hard won Flynn Family secrets?"

Eric managed to look chagrined. "That was the general idea."

Danni made a tsking sound. "That's not the way it goes down. You have to earn it. Work for it."

His hand slid to her hip, sending a shocking thrill through her system.

"And not like that, although I like where your head's at," she told him with a smile.

"But you do know how to do it?" he asked, though it didn't sound like a question.

"Sure, my dad taught me when I was twelve. He'd give me ice cream when I won."

Eric shook his head. "My dad was coaching my baseball team when I was twelve." A tad judgmental perhaps.

"Actually, counting cards teaches valuable math skills." She spotted the free deck of cards the casino provided on his nightstand. She sat up and reached for them, opening the package. "Observe," she said as she laid the cards out on the bed before him. The sheet slipped down below her breasts, and she yanked the material higher before continuing. "Aces, tens and face cards you give a value of negative one. Two through six, positive one. Everything else is a zero. When you get a pair, you do the math."

"Seems easy enough," he said, tugging at the sheet. Her nipples hardened, clearly visible in spite of the bunched-up expensive cotton.

"Do you want me to teach you or not?" she asked, her voice firm, but a smile in her eyes.

He didn't answer right away, his eyes watchful as he brought the sheet lower.

"I'm thinking," he said after a moment.

"Learning the technique is always easy."

His eyes told her he found a double meaning in her words. "Do you want to learn this or practice your...technique?"

"I want to learn this *and* practice my technique." He raised the sheet, effectively hiding her breasts once more. "We'll practice afterwards."

Even when he teased her, this man left her breathless. She forced herself to be serious. "Learning the technique is easy...putting it into practice, that's where the effort, art and patience come in. Effort because you have to memorize every possible card combination. Art because you got to look like you're not doing it. Patience because it can take a long time to get to the winning combination and you can only bet on plus two or higher. Even with the count in your favor, you won't always win."

"I plan to win," he said, his eyes meeting hers.

Her insides got all quivery. "That's the perfect con attitude. Don't forget that the casino is going to try and distract you. Get you drunk. Draw your attention to the waitresses with huge boobs."

"Noted. Hire women with big racks."

Danni laughed and lightly punched Eric in the shoulder. "What I'm saying is, be steady. Be focused."

"I think I got it. You ready to play?"

"I'm always ready to play. Care to make it interesting?" she asked. There she went again. Would that phrase ever leave her, or was it just ingrained into her DNA?

He arched a brow. "How interesting are we talking?"

"Well, you won't have much of an edge playing here with me with nothing to lose. You're a man who likes to be in control. How about this—you lose, I tie you up and do all kinds of things to your body."

His hesitation was her answer. Suddenly, she didn't feel so lighthearted. "You trust me, don't you, Eric?" she asked, hating that touch of vulnerability in her voice.

A wicked grin formed on his lips. "I tie you up if I win."

"Done," she said, excitement already leaping within her.

CASSIE OPENED HER OFFICE after lunch and scanned her list of appointments. She had a full afternoon. Good. She'd need them to keep her mind off Dirk. What had she been thinking? Why would she stay and talk to him in her backyard?

Now she was beginning to crave second helpings. *Leftovers only caused indigestion.* She'd written that at some point. Hadn't she?

Her cell phone rang, and she fished it out of her purse. The device was reserved for urgent matters with her patients. "Hello."

"Wanted to make sure you got there safe."

Her heartbeat quickened at the sound of Dirk's voice, but for a different reason. "Why would you care?"

"I protect what's mine."

"Then you've wasted your time because I am not yours, Mr. Archaic." There'd been a time she would have cherished his words.

"Oh, you've always been mine, Cassie. Even when I was stupid. And if it makes you feel better, I'm yours. You can be archaic right along with me."

A possessiveness returned that she'd not felt in a long time, but she forced herself to laugh. "I'm liking the stupid part. Everything else…meh."

"What are you doing right now?" he asked, his voice pitched low. A bedroom voice.

"Hanging up."

"No, that doesn't work. You're too eager to hear what I'm going to say next."

She sucked in a breath and bit her lip to keep from screaming. Cassie hated it when this man was right. He was supposed to be wrong. All the time wrong.

"Slip your hand under your blouse. When we were sitting at the table last night, all I could think about this morning were your breasts."

"That must be why you didn't make any sense."

"Tell me how soft your skin feels. Touch your nipples."

The nipples in question hardened.

For one tempting moment, she gave in to the thrill of her body responding. "You're supposed to be conducting an investigation of the tape, not trying to seduce me."

"Why can't I do both? I want to see you again," he murmured. Memories of the first time he'd asked her on a date surfaced. The man on the phone was a very different person from the shy boy who'd met her outside her locker.

"Maybe we can go out sometime?" the boy from her past had asked.

"Maybe what I want to do is smack you on the ass," the woman of the present told him.

"Maybe I'm into that."

And despite herself…she laughed. In the face of wanting to hate this man more than any person who walked the earth—and drive him away—she felt a tiny chink of the iron she'd encased her heart in break away.

Then images of her sex tape flashed through her mind. Did she want a new little audio to go right next to the download button? "I am on my cell phone. This is not going to happen. I am not about to have phone sex on an easily recordable cell phone at the same time my sex tape can be had online twenty-four seven."

"Phone sex? Is that what you're suggesting? The thought never entered my mind. Cassie, you've grown so wicked." His tone was the epitome of shocked innocence. "I like it," he said.

Cassie closed her eyes and shook her head to clear it of desire. "You know you were aiming for a little phone sex."

"So you'd be up for it after the tape is off the Internet?" he asked.

Cassie sucked in a calming breath. "Not with you," she replied between clenched teeth. "How did you get my cell number anyway?"

"Your mother."

What part of emergency did Mom not understand?

"Don't call me again. Not unless it's to tell me you know who stole our tape," she said, deciding at that moment that she believed him when he said he wasn't involved in their tape being on the Internet.

"Then I'll be calling soon."

Did he already know something? "What? Tell me," she urged.

"Not until I have a name."

Cassie could literally hear the laughter in his voice as Dirk hung up the phone. What happened to the nice, sweet boy who lived next door?

Oh, yeah, that's right. He grew up and became a man. Cassie frowned. She was not a man hater. Just a one-man hater, and he was still bothering her.

DANNI'S CELL CHIRPED as Eric lost another round. "You're really terrible at cheating," she told him as she scrambled for her phone.

Eric didn't seem fazed by her taunt. "Maybe it's the teacher."

She made a face at him as she answered the phone. "Hello."

"It's Cassie. I could really use a drink. Not coffee," she said all at once.

Danni pulled the sheet higher across her breasts as Eric dealt the next round. "Uh, I'm trying to tie up some loose ends right now." *Yeah, he'd be tied up before long.*

"Tomorrow, then. Dirk's called me."

"Really?" Now this was starting to get interesting. Not as interesting as the lazy circles Eric was tracing along her thigh. Normally she'd congratulate him on devising a strategy that might help him win a hand or two. He made an awesome diversion.

"It's a date. I can't wait to hear all about it," Danni said as she hung up.

"You already making another date while here with me?" Eric asked, looking sexy and rumpled with the sheets twisted around him.

"A gal's got to keep all her options open," she said. "That was Cassie, she's back here in Reno. We were setting up a time to gab." She stroked his chest, loving the play of his muscles under her fingers. "I need a bit more fodder about you before I see her tomorrow."

He lifted an eyebrow, bunching the pillow under his head. "What's this about tying up loose ends?"

"You have any ties stashed around here?" she asked. Her corporate lover dressed business casual. No ties in sight. He looked relaxed now…

Eric angled his head toward a closet. "In there. Why?"

Danni made a point to look at the stack of cards on the bed. "Because you're losing, and it's time to pay up."

"There's still a fourth of the cards left in the stack," he said.

Danni nodded. "True. But even if you magically developed the skill to count the remaining cards, believe me when I tell you, statistically you're not going to win. All the high cards are gone. I'm thinking four ties should do it."

With a wink, Eric shoved the cards onto the floor and reclined against the pillows.

Her system instantly reacted to his open invitation for her to handle his body. "Now wait a minute. This is supposed to be your punishment. Don't look so excited."

"I have a hot, sexy woman who is going to do all kinds of things to me. I only have to be here and enjoy it. I don't even have to put forth the effort of foreplay. I'm thinking I won."

Danni placed her hands on her hips. "Now you're taking liberties, and ruining my fun."

Eric imitated the face of someone who was bored. "Please. Don't hurt me," he pleaded, his voice monotone, but laughter shone in his eyes.

Danni yanked the ties off the hanger and stalked to the bed. She'd show him. He wouldn't enjoy this. Much. Her body hummed with excitement.

Grabbing his right arm, she secured one end of the tie around his wrist, and the other to the headboard. She did the same to his left arm. His feet were a little

more tricky as there was no footboard, but she impro-
vised with the bed frame.

"Bed manufacturers are just making it more and
more complicated to tie someone up these days," she
said, straightening.

"Done this a lot, have you?"

"No, but luckily I was a Scout, so I know my way
around a knot. Honestly, you're my first time, so you'll
have to forgive me if I make any wrong moves."

"You haven't made one yet."

Danni lightly ran her fingers along his skin, loving
his hot-blooded reaction to her touch. Danni scooted
onto the bed and straddled him, and their gazes locked.
This was going to be amazing.

AN HOUR AND A HALF LATER, they were both dressed in
robes and sitting cross-legged on the bed, eating a late-
night snack courtesy of room service.

"There at the end, before you had your way with
me, I was getting the hang of card counting," he said.

"It takes practice. It still didn't make sense for you
to make a bet over it. There are rules about betting, too.
I should teach you the Kelly formula," she offered as
she tucked a chip into her mouth.

"The Reynolds formula is that I don't bet anything
that I'm not prepared to lose."

Her breath hitched at the knowledge that Eric liked
the idea of her tying him up.

"Card counting is a dying art, at least in casino
play. With shoes that hold up to six decks at a time,

there's no way a person can calculate everything in their head now."

"We evil security chiefs."

Danni's back straightened as a thought occurred to her. "Unless we steal a shoe."

Eric shuddered. "Couldn't happen."

"Ah, but you don't know the stories some tell around the campfire," she said and grinned from ear to ear. "The skill is still important. I can spot trends in the cards by using it, and that makes learning the technique worth your while."

"So, do you really know some sleight-of-hand tricks?" he asked between bites of his sandwich.

She nodded and took a drink of water. "I'll show you the very first thing my father ever taught me. It'll be good for you to know here at the casino. See that white packet of sugar on the tray the waiter brought? Pretend that's a betting chip. Hand me one of those blue packets. Now watch."

She tucked the blue packet into her palm. "If I think I should change the bet, I do something like this." With a quick wave, the blue packet was now where the white packet had been. The white packet was gone.

"And see…I can do the reverse. Or add a packet so I have both chips."

Eric whistled. "That was quick."

"This is a trick an advantage gambler would use when the pit boss is somewhere else. A tired, bored and inattentive dealer is an advantage gambler's best friend. I could also palm weighted or magnetized dice at the craps

table with a sleight-of-hand move. Works even better if you have someone who can provide a distraction."

"You provide a *distraction*. I'll never see that wall by my door the same way again."

Danni almost giggled. *Gawd. What had she turned into?* She shifted to instruction mode to keep herself focused. "You know, there's a phrase about a wall in conning. Playing someone against the wall is when you take a mark into a real setting. Like a bank, or hotel room."

Eric grew absolutely still. "Oh, yeah? Any others I should know?" he asked.

She nodded, clearly into the topic. "There's also giving the convincer. That's when you give in to your mark a bit, so they think they're on to a good thing."

Her face heated. Eric had slipped her a great convincer. Her glance cut to his face. His lips were twisting as if he'd read her mind and knew where her dirty thoughts had headed.

She made a play of fanning herself. "Didn't realize how sexual these phrases could sound," she said, donning her Southern accent.

"Good accent."

Danni couldn't hide her rueful smile. "I know a lot."

The telephone beside the bed began to ring. He glanced at the caller ID. His expression grew dim. "I've got to take this."

"No problem," she said as she scooted off the bed. Danni walked toward the large window so Eric would have some privacy. Eric's suite was on one of the

highest floors, and it gave a great view of the mountains surrounding Reno. The day had been practically cloudless and tonight's view was outstanding. She didn't take great views for granted.

She smiled, thinking of the great views Eric provided. Not just of his sexy body, but of a future. How she'd longed to have a normal relationship with someone she liked and respected and could be completely honest with. Eric was interested in her, not judgmental of her past, and cared about her. Plus, he made her laugh. He was a man she could easily fall for. Daydream about. Become a sap for.

Her heart wasn't playing around here. This was serious. The breath caught in her chest, but these new realizations didn't scare her. Nor did she have some weird desire to mess it all up so she wouldn't look like a sucker in the end.

A moment later, she felt Eric's hands at her shoulders. "Looks like I have to go downstairs. A pit boss issue."

Had to be big if the pit boss wanted him down there. She was surprised by the wave of disappointment she felt at the news. She didn't consciously allow herself to depend on someone who could disappoint her. Somehow Eric had slipped in. "I'll get my things."

"Stay here if you want," he ventured, turning her to face him. He caressed her cheek with the back of his hand. "Spend the night. It's late, and I don't like the idea of you driving alone to your apartment."

Danni grew warm and tingly, not from the heat of his

hands on her body, but from his words. Few people had cared about her well-being the way Eric did.

She should feel ridiculous. A grown woman who'd been on her own for years, taking pleasure in the protector role Eric had adopted. After all, she'd shown she could take care of herself. But Eric had been like that since their first date. She remembered him checking her door to make sure it was locked.

Usually, she'd distrusted that kind of behavior, but now Danni liked it. She welcomed the rightness of it. Lovers should want to take care of each other. Protect one another. She felt that way about him.

She stretched on her tiptoes and gave him one hot kiss, loving the taste of him. Relishing the sensation of how nice it was to be familiar with the texture of his lips, but knowing she had a lot more to explore about this man. "I'd like to stay," she said.

A wicked gleam entered his brown eyes. "After that kiss…I'll hurry back." They walked hand in hand to the bed, where she settled with the room service meal in front of her. She watched Eric change clothes as she finished her sandwich. With another kiss, she was alone in his suite. Welcomed by him. Trusted by him. It was a great feeling.

And she made a vow that she wouldn't snoop.

ERIC SHOVED HIS HANDS into his pockets and made quick time to the elevator. He was in real trouble here. This went way beyond casual. He was really starting to like Danni. He'd never expected to fall for her.

That phone call from downstairs couldn't have come at a better time. He needed to get back on track. An unruly drunk tourist causing a disturbance was far preferable to having to face what was going on in his personal life.

Personal life? He didn't have a personal life. He had work. He had female acquaintances. And he had more work.

Maybe after this stint was done. Maybe…

No. He was here to do a job. And that was all it would be. Could ever be.

11

ERIC TRIED TO WAKE HER UP with a kiss. She snuggled deeper into the pillow. Morning person Danni was not. Then her fuddled brain realized this was Eric. *Trying to wake her up with a kiss.* She rolled over and smiled. His beautiful brown eyes snapped into focus.

Danni reached for him, wanting to bring his big body down beside her. He resisted her attempts to draw him into the warm bed. "You have class this morning."

And with those words she shot straight up, her gaze searching for a clock. How could she have stayed the whole night? She'd completely sold out to sleep. Didn't even remember him coming back to bed.

"We have enough time to take a shower," he said in a tone that would corrupt any nice girl. Which she wasn't.

She stopped her frantic search and met his eyes instead. "We?" she asked, her body instantly reacting to his words. She noticed Eric still wore the clothes he'd dressed in last night before he left.

"Poor baby, you had to work all night," she said, loving the concern she felt. Concern for a lover was normal after all, and she was really loving all aspects of normalcy.

Strain tightened the skin around his eyes. "There were some details to work out," he said.

"All good now?" she asked.

His gaze left hers as he stood. "It's all on track again."

Danni surged to her knees, twining her arms around his neck. She wanted to get his mind off of business and back on, well, *business.* "So, you were saying something about a shower…" She let her voice trail off as she licked the spot under his ear she knew he liked. A lot.

His arms surrounded her, and he hauled her closer up against his chest. "I've been thinking about soaping your entire body."

Her skin became tingly. "I'm feeling really, really dirty. Especially my breasts. They'll need a lot of soap."

His brown eyes darkened, and he swooped her up into his arms and carted her into the bathroom. Danni shoved his shirt off his body as his hands drew sighing responses from her. Soon she had him naked and wet beneath the steam of the shower, and Eric got her very, very clean.

Afterward, she sat revived and cross-legged on his bed wearing her floral skirt and shirt from the night before. She'd have just enough time to stop by her apartment and change. But first she'd have to tackle the tangles from her hair using his comb. She'd have to discreetly tuck a bottle of conditioner into her purse. Just in case something like this ever happened again.

Eric sat down beside her, and Danni looked up because his body felt tight beside her. Like every muscle he possessed was tensed.

"It occurred to me that you were stuck in here last night," he said, his expression neutral, his tone offhand. "I made you a keycard, in case something like that happened again."

He held out the piece of plastic toward her.

"A keycard to your room?" she asked, probably sounding as silly as she felt asking something so obvious. Even though excitement raced through her, she was so, so surprised.

He nodded, making a liar of his nonchalant demeanor from before. "Only if you want it."

Danni smiled, taking the key from him. "I'd like that. You're a fast mover," she said, her tone light and teasing, despite the fact that they'd moved into the realm of commitment.

"Believe me, I've never moved this fast," he said, chagrined.

She dropped the comb, her gaze seeking out his. "Really?" she asked. Her heartbeat quickened. This was important. Why did this feel like one of the most important questions of her life? Five days ago she'd never even known this man. Today she couldn't imagine beginning her day without thinking of him. It was crazy.

He caught her chin, tipping her face upward. "Yes, really," he said, his expression telling her it was the truth and even he seemed surprised by it.

Eric lowered his lips and kissed her. She found his kiss not a sexual, I'm-about-to-have-you-right-now kind of kiss, but one of promise and frank candor. *I like you. I want to spend my time with you.*

Then his tongue caressed the seam of her lips, and that frank candor added *I crave you*.

Eric broke off the kiss, resting his forehead against hers, the sound of their breathing the only sound. "Now go," he said. His voice once again held a teasing edge. "You have class, and between work and your hot body, I'm exhausted."

She laughed and then slid off the bed. Eric lifted the covers and settled between the sheets with a sigh. Danni slid into her shoes, grabbed her new keycard, and with a kiss turned off the light.

"Good night."

She felt his gaze on her all the way to the door.

CASSIE GLARED at her watch, and knocked on Danni's apartment door again. Danni was late. Strange, since Danni was notorious for always being on time. Probably a side effect from her incarceration all those years ago.

Cassie was about to drag out her cell phone when Danni breezed up the staircase, despite dragging her steno case along with her. Her best friend practically vibrating happiness, cheerfulness and…and…Cassie could barely think it. Like a woman in love.

Danni came around the corner, and the smile said it all. Definitely a woman in love.

"Tell me you haven't slept with him?" Cassie asked her, dreading the answer. If Danni had, she'd have broken nearly every *Kiss…But Confirm* rule Cassie stressed in her book.

Danni's eyes widened and pink tinted her cheeks. "How did you know? Is it that obvious?"

Cassie nodded. "Even having been found out, you still have that big smile on your face."

Her friend grew flustered, dropping her keys. "Can we wait to have the safe sex talk inside, *Mom?*" Danni joked, trying to sound frustrated, but clearly not.

Bending, Cassie retrieved the keys, and unlocked the door, and the two entered Danni's apartment.

They'd found this furnished efficiency apartment together. Danni couldn't afford much on her waitress salary, and with no furniture to speak of, the place had been perfect. Over time, Danni had discovered she possessed an eclectic style. Cassie liked how Danni managed to make a combination of the modern funky prints on the walls, animal skin throw pillows and Americana sofa circa 1960 work.

Cassie plopped herself on that sofa now. "Okay, I'm listening."

Danni set her steno machine case on the black-and-chrome retro table in her kitchen. "We didn't plan it. It sort of happened. I was pointing out an advantage gambler, and the next thing we're pinned against the wall in his suite. We've only known each other a week. Do you think that's too fast?"

Horrendously. "No," Cassie lied.

"I mean, I know what you're going to say. I broke your rules. Minimum of three months before sex. Nothing less than a full background check."

"Google is a girl's best friend," Cassie said, the cynicism coming out loud and clear.

Danni pulled her steno machine from the case and began to type. "I don't even care that I don't know where he graduated from high school or even anything remotely personal about him. Last night was just so right. Has been from that first time I met him."

"Wait a minute. You're not transcribing our conversation? I hate it when you do that."

"You hate it even more when you have to read drills to me. I'm falling behind in my machine shorthand class. I was less than seventy percent accurate today, and I can't pass at that rate."

"Okay, but all potentially embarrassing conversation will be from you."

"I'll give you the paper when I'm done. You can burn it."

Cassie nodded. "Back to Eric. What was he like this morning?" That was the true test.

If possible, Danni's smile widened. "He gave me the key to his suite."

In all the years she'd known her, Cassie had never seen Danni so happy. Why was Cassie being so mean? She reached over and patted her friend on the hand. "Actually, you're lucky when things happen that easily."

Danni let out a deep breath, as if she'd been nervous to tell Cassie everything. She was being a bad friend. Danni had turned her life around—she deserved some happiness. Cassie gave Danni a big smile.

"This is the first time I've ever been truly honest

with a man. Not only did he not reject me, he's encouraged me."

"That's the way it's supposed to be. Okay, you have my official approval."

Danni laughed. "For that, I'll even make you dinner later. Tell me how everything went with Dirk."

Cassie slumped against the sofa.

"That bad, huh? How'd he look?"

Cassie swallowed. Her first love looked better than ever. Damn him. "Great," she said.

"That's too bad."

"He should have looked bad. Been married. Anything." She began to fidget with the black fringe from the sofa pillow.

"Now this is sounding interesting," Danni said, able to keep typing, converse and never look in Cassie's direction. "Are you still attracted to him?"

Oh, God, yes. "Maybe," Cassie hedged. At this her friend looked up. She met Danni's eyes. "He said he still thinks about me. Has never forgotten me." *The jerk.*

"Hey, that's great."

Cassie's answer was silence.

"Isn't it?" she asked, still not returning to her typing.

Cassie knocked a magazine onto the floor, and she took her time picking it up. Avoidance. When had she taken up that trick? Danni just glared at her expectantly.

"You know that love you have when you're seventeen. It's so pure and earnest, and you think you're going to die if you don't have that person. And then they love you back and it's like a whole new beautiful

world awakens filled with rainbows and sunshine and birds singing."

"Come to think of it, I noticed the birds singing this morning."

"Well, back away friend because one day Prince Charming says maybe it's time we should see other people. Just to make sure. And then he comes home with his new slut girlfriend, and you're too heartbroken to remember your sex tape."

"Was he the one who put the tape on the Internet?"

"He says not, and I believe him. In fact, he's going to search out who did it. He told me that last night in my backyard."

"Backyard? I thought you were meeting him at a restaurant."

"I did, but later he came by to tell me he would find out who put the tape up on the Internet."

Danni returned to typing and raised an eyebrow. "And for that he *had* to tell you in person. What's going on here?"

Cassie sank her forehead on her hands. "I don't know. For a moment last night, all I could think of was how easy it would be to kiss him. Be with him. We used to fit. A near perfect match, in fact."

"The sex I saw on that tape didn't really…match."

"We'd both been virgins learning together. Given the chance, we would have worked that out in time, too." Which made Dirk's assertion that he was better at love-making all the more tempting because no one had ever turned her on, touched who she was the way Dirk had.

Immediately her skin remembered every touch, every caress, every emotion this man ever gave her.

He'd said he was better at it now. Her body suddenly wanted to find out the truth. She sucked in a breath. "He says he still wants me. And for a moment, I wanted him, too."

"Then try to remember that you're a woman. He's a man. You both want to hook up. Forget everything else and hook up."

Cassie shook her head and glanced at Danni. "It's not that easy. He hurt me like nothing else ever did. I feel like I should punish him over and over and over."

"Have you thought that maybe that's not the most healthy path for you to follow?"

"No, and I'm not going to. My first book was based on the premise of finding a healthy relationship while still hating the person who broke your heart."

Danni's face turned hopeful. "So, maybe you can have a relationship with the person who can mend your heart. Write a new book."

Wasn't there a saying about happy in love people being the most annoying? "I don't want a relationship with him."

"Then we're back to the hook-up scenario. Use him for sex."

"Oh, those are famous last words. Half my clients end up hooked permanently with the man they were only going to use for sex."

"Then use him for closure. Whatever. You still obviously have him in your system."

"I thought you were going to feed me," Cassie said, ready to try avoidance again. But to tell the truth, that closure system cleanse scenario didn't sound half bad.

12

THE WAY ERIC FIGURED IT, Danni would probably have two reactions to his offer. No and hell no. In fact, that's what he would like her to say. What he feared was that she would say yes.

They were back to Sunday night because of her work schedule at the diner. He'd love to get her out of that job.

"You look beautiful," he told her as she met him at the fancy Italian restaurant in the hotel.

Danni smiled, and glanced down at the wispy black dress with the cutouts. Cutouts that gave him a flash of hidden skin whenever she moved. The woman could drive a man crazy.

"Thanks. I had to borrow the outfit from Cassie. My wardrobe doesn't extend to simple black slip dresses."

There was her honesty again. For the first time Eric felt guilty. Why, he didn't know. He had a job to do. Emotions didn't factor into work. He'd been careful. Yet, reluctance was there.

"I got you something," he said to break him from those unproductive thoughts.

Her smile widened, and she leaned forward in anticipation. "Are there any sweeter words than those?"

Reaching into his pocket, he pulled out a black ID cardholder and lanyard. It matched his. She looked up at him in confusion.

"I've lined up some consulting work for you at the casino, if you're interested. It would give you better hours than at the restaurant."

This late evening date wasn't the first time they'd had to work around her schedule in the last week. They'd seen each other every night since he'd given her his key. Eric pushed the cardholder across the table toward her.

"What would I be doing?" She fingered the lanyard string as if she didn't know how to react. Had he made this proposal too soon?

"Walking the casino floor. Writing down your observations. Maybe a few sessions with the pit bosses."

She took a deep breath. "Ahhh, to never fill drink orders again. Never balance five salad plates at a time. No more cranky, hungry customers. I could almost tap-dance on the dinner table."

He felt the need to warn her off. "On the other hand, being in a casino, surrounded by dozens of tempting money-making opportunities…" His words trailed off, letting her fill in the blanks.

"Hmm," she said, a frown marring her forehead. He almost willed her to say no. But then, he had to make things work at the casino.

"You'd also have to work on a one-on-one basis with me," he said.

"Sounds pretty rough."

He winked at her. "I think you can handle it."

"I'll turn in my notice tomorrow."

He nodded, not wanting to acknowledge his disappointment. He'd fully expected her agreement all along—the offer was too good. "We'll have to get pictures for your name badge. But I want you to hide it at first so that you look like an ordinary gambler. I want to see if security notices anything."

"Sounds covert. And fun. I did plenty of covert kinds of recon with my da—"

His hand stilled as he was reaching for his water glass. "Go on. It's okay to talk about your father."

She gave a dismissive shrug. "It was nothing. That's behind me. I only wanted you to know the covert side of this job would be easy breezy."

He glanced away. "Sometimes covert isn't always what it's cracked up to be."

She opened her mouth as if to question him further about his comment. But suddenly he didn't want to think about his job, or Danni's past, nor her father. Right now he only wanted to be with her. To hold her. Smell her hair. She felt right in his life. Her eyes followed him as he walked around their table toward her. Gently, he drew her up beside him. "Dance with me," he urged.

He led her away from their table, and she pressed herself close to him, as if she liked being in his arms as much as he liked her there.

Tonight he didn't want to be Eric Reynolds, head of casino security or anything else for that matter. Tonight he'd be the man who adored Danni.

Maybe that would be enough.

TWO DAYS LATER, Danni found herself walking the floor, the facade of green gambler surrounding her entire body. She made mental notes of when the staff grew bored, what occurrences drew their attention and received a hot kiss when she handed in her typed report to Eric. She loved being secure in his arms and warm in the knowledge that this man trusted her. More importantly, she'd earned his trust.

She pledged a vow right then. Temptation of the casino or not, she'd make herself be the kind of person who deserved someone like Eric Reynolds.

Today her job was to see which dealers she could distract. She'd gone with flashy and low-cut. She sidled up to a young male dealer.

"Is this a high stakes table?" she asked, her voice sexy. "I need someone who'll go easy on me."

To his credit, the dealer merely blinked at her not-so-subtle but innocently delivered sexual innuendo.

"The casino offers many 'how-to' classes," he said, no-nonsense. With one quick glance at her cleavage, the dealer returned his attention to the game.

With a smile, she walked on. That dealer had passed her first simple test.

"Laying it on a little thick with that Southern drawl, aren't you? Surely I taught you better than that."

Danni spun on her heel to face her father eye-to-eye. Frustration and disappointment at seeing him here deprived her of the sense of accomplishment she'd begun to find in her job.

She dropped her expression of sweet Southern lady

and tugged her dad by the arm into a corner. "How'd you get in here? The security at the front door would have recognized you for sure."

"Tell your boyfriend his front door staff is weak." His tone was playfully mocking.

Danni gasped. "How did you find out about Eric?"

Daniel Flynn shook his head. "Danni-bear, when are you going to stop underestimating your old man? Aren't you happy to see me?"

Guilt instantly assailed her. "Of course I am. Let me grab my purse and we can get out of here. I'll take you to lunch," she said, reaching for his arm to draw him outside. Outside and very far away.

Her father stayed planted to the carpet. He gave the interior of the casino the once-over. "Nice gig you've got going here."

She could imagine the opportunistic wheels begin to spin in her father's head. No, not now. Why'd her dad have to show up when things were finally going so right in her life?

Danni shrugged, shooting for nonchalant. "It pays the bills. In fact, I'll pay for lunch with my paycheck. Think of it as one more way to get money from a casino."

Daniel's eyes met hers, his expression serious. After her mother died, her father had only been serious about one thing. Money. "I have access to plenty of money from a casino, you know that. Just need a wee bit to get it out."

Danni swallowed. Her father had just mentioned the

one thing they never spoke of. Ever. She glanced around, paranoid someone would hear him.

"What's the rest of their protection like here?" he asked, casual, like he wasn't about to ask his daughter to help him rip off the casino where her boyfriend was the head of security.

"No," she said firmly.

Surprise blanketed his face. People rarely told him no. She'd never had occasion to be so forceful with her father, and the sensation of it felt foreign to her. Behind her back, Danni began twisting her fingers together.

He scanned the layout of the room as if he hadn't heard her, his examination more calculating this time. "I think my best shot will be at craps. Be a dear and borrow a pair of their dice, would you?"

It was always borrow. Never steal. Another of the Flynn Family coping techniques. Anguish tore at her heart. She couldn't lose everything that she'd gained. Her father could ruin it all.

"No, Dad, I won't help you do it. You shouldn't even be here. You're violating your parole." She dug a finger into his chest. "You promised me you'd go straight this time. Didn't you read the brochures I brought you from the horticulture program?"

He shifted easily from one foot to the other, as if he were anxious to get started. Anxious to destroy what she'd begun to build. "I'll have plenty of time to do that after I get my money. You know that, Danni. You've always known I wasn't going to leave it with the Swiss. I've waited for a long time."

She sucked in a breath. Danni gave an uncomfortable sideways glance, making sure there were no curious eyes or ears close by. Casino security was state-of-the-art. She'd witnessed it herself now in her new role here.

"I don't know what you're talking about," she said.

Her father reached out and grabbed her around the arm. "The dice, Danni. You owe me that."

"Is there a problem?"

Relief and guilt assailed her. Relief because that strong reassuring voice was Eric's. Guilt because she knew her father was right. She owed him.

Daniel dropped his hand from her arm, and stuck his hand toward Eric to shake.

"Eric, this is my father, Daniel Flynn." She strove for easygoing, even though she was introducing the head of casino security to a man who could be one of the most notorious flimflam men to grace Nevada. "Dad, Eric Reynolds."

The two men shook hands, and Danni quickly searched Eric's face for any signs of alarm or disgust. Instead, he only appeared tired and weary. Her urge to smooth the hair from his face and caress his cheek felt normal. Yes. Perhaps she wasn't overreacting and making a scene right now. Although she felt there was a huge neon sign above her head proclaiming thief—don't trust.

"Nice to meet you, but I must be off." Daniel gave her a kiss to the temple. "Remember what we talked about. I'll need that by Friday."

"What's with Friday?" Eric asked after her father

sauntered out of earshot, his expression momentarily fierce.

She shrugged. "Nothing. My father asked me for a favor, but I told him no can do."

"You okay?" he asked, back to being her gentle lover.

She nodded, plastering on a smile. "Fine. Sometimes my dad can be…over-the-top. Listen, I should explain—"

Eric gently placed his finger over her lips. "You don't have to. You told me your father's name before. And I alerted the front door staff that he may show up here."

She blinked in surprise. "You did? How did you know?"

"I googled you."

The idea of Eric googling her the way Cassie had suggested so many times struck her as so funny that it took her a moment to stop laughing.

Then she realized Eric had been so thoughtful he actually cleared her father's entrance into the casino. For her. Oh, he probably had posted a notice for an available security staff person to follow her father's every step to make sure no money "left" the casino, but Eric's gesture was so overwhelming that all laughter faded.

"You're really great, you know that?" she said, as she threaded her fingers through his.

"All part of the service," he noted, lowering his head, his scent surrounding her.

"You kiss me too much in here and my cover will be blown in front of the staff. They'll know I'm working for you."

Eric shook his head, but his eyes didn't meet hers. "That won't matter much longer anyway."

She loved him.

The thought hit her so quickly and so suddenly she forgot to ask him why it wouldn't matter about the staff knowing she was his girlfriend. And it scared her.

What she felt for him was not a this-is-love…time-to-get-dysfunctional. More of a this-is-love…WOW. Enjoy it. She planned to enjoy it right now.

"I have a break coming up," she said, shooting for seductive in her tone.

Sensual darkness filled his eyes. "I think I can work a business meeting in my suite into the schedule."

CASSIE'S LAST APPOINTMENT had already left, and she was settling down to perform her favorite task of the day—straightening up her desk. Her receptionist buzzed in as she was aligning her notepads.

"There's a man here to see you," Heather said.

Cassie glanced up at the clock over the door. Sometimes she could fit in walk-ins. Relationship trouble didn't follow a nine-to-five schedule. But tonight Cassie had an appointment at a day spa, and she was up for some glam time.

"Sorry, Heather. Make an appointment. I can't fit him in today."

"He says it's personal. Something about a tape on the Internet."

Dirk.

The man was like a bad penny. Bad everything. And

yet her body still hungered for him as if he held the source for chocolate.

She sighed in resignation. "Okay, let him in, and please lock up."

"You don't want me to stay?" Heather asked. For safety reasons, it was policy Cassie never stayed alone in the office.

"No, it's okay. This is someone I knew from high school." Even though the effort was wasted on Dirk, Cassie smoothed her hair and straightened her skirt, the soft hum of anticipation buzzing in her blood.

The doorknob turned and Dirk walked through the door. Jeans, T-shirt. A million men wore those same items every day. None of those guys looked half as good as Dirk did right now. Entering her office. Invading her personal space. She shrank back against her chair.

His steps slowed as he saw her, and a smile spread across his rugged face. "I like you in your counselor uniform."

Cassie glanced down at her plain black skirt, sensible shoes and white V-neck blouse. With her hair in a knot on the top of her head it could definitely be classified as the uniform she wore to work.

Dirk shut the door behind him. "I think I'm on to something with the tape. You remember that roommate I had second semester of our sophomore year?"

She had a vague image in her mind—blond, short, hair already thinning. The type of man prone to a large gut by the time he was thirty. She nodded.

"What was his name?" Dirk asked.

She couldn't remember. "He was such a jerk you moved out after only a couple of weeks."

Dirk nodded. "That's right. I can't remember his name either. I think maybe if we watch the tape together, it might remind us."

"You think he's the one?" she asked, trying to ignore the hardening of her nipples at his suggestion of viewing the tape together.

"I'm almost positive. He had a thing for you."

Cassie shuddered. "Yuck. Why'd you have to tell me that? The guy was so creepy." Her whole body revolted as she remembered the spine-chilling way the guy used to follow her with his eyes. Twice she spotted him skulking outside one of her classes.

"And the kind of guy who'd steal another man's things."

With a heavy sigh, Cassie jiggled the mouse to wake up her computer, then typed in the Web site with their lovemaking uploaded on it. She didn't want to do this, but if watching this could jog their memories of this guy's name, and getting the tape back, she'd do it.

After a few moments, the image of her naked breasts filled the screen. Dirk's sexy backside was clearly visible as he kissed and licked her nipples.

Man, he'd been good at that.

Her breasts grew heavy and her nipples hardened at the remembered pleasure.

A moan escaped from the woman on the screen. Her.

"Was that fake?" Dirk asked behind her, so close she felt the heat from his body.

Her breathing shallowed. "No," she said.

"You ready?" the taped Dirk asked, and the taped Cassie responded by wrapping her arms around his neck and her legs around his waist.

In real life, the back of her neck began to tingle. She was reliving that moment from so many years ago. Reliving it as if it were happening right now.

Cassie was doing very intimate things on the tape, and standing beside the very man with whom she'd been doing those intimate things. She didn't feel detached. She felt very, very involved.

Her muscles tensed. Her skin grew warm.

Stage One of Sexual Desire. Soon her pupils would dilate and the walls of her vagina would grow slick.

Stage Two.

Then she'd grab him by the shoulders and do him.

She seized the mouse and hit the red button on the window of the Web site, sending the sounds and sights away. "I've seen the tape. Seeing it together isn't going to help us."

Dirk turned toward her, the teasing look on his face vanished. Instead, raw hunger dwelled in his eyes. Raw hunger for her.

Something deep and elemental inside her responded.

She'd placed herself in a position only inches away from him when she'd yanked for the mouse. They were so close. With a groan, he pulled her fully into his arms. She met his mouth with ready abandon.

She should make herself stop. Tear herself away. But she didn't.

Cassie was desperate to discover everything new and old about Dirk's body. How he'd changed. How he was the same. She ran her hands up the muscles on his back. No shy, exploring girl. She touched him as a woman touched a man. The caress of a woman who wanted that man very much.

Her breathing grew harsh, her movements frantic. Cassie could think of nothing but getting Dirk's shirt off his chest, and just how fast she could do it. She grabbed the bottom of his T-shirt and yanked it hard out of the waistband of his jeans. He followed suit, in too much of a hurry to fully remove her blouse—just unbuttoning it and smoothing the silky material to the side. Thankfully the bra had a front clasp.

Dirk shoved the papers on her desk aside and she scooted onto the top, her legs dangling at the knees. He followed her down, balancing his full weight on his forearms.

She twined her arms around his neck the same way she had on the tape, sinking her fingers into the silkiness of his hair. The weight of him on her body made her ache. The hard bulge of his erection made contact with all the right places.

His hand traveled up her thigh, pushing her skirt out of his way as he went. He found the barrier of her panties, and stopped.

She opened her eyes to see Dirk's strained expression.

"Cassie, tell me you want me," he said, his voice little more than a ragged groan.

Disappointment took away some of the sensual

haze. Why did he have to talk? Why did he have to bring her to reality, make her acknowledge what she was feeling? A moment ago, she could have had raw, animalistic sex on the top of her desk with Dirk and written it off as heat of the moment.

Now, because he asked her to voice what she sought, she couldn't write their sex off as anything but that she was a woman who wanted him.

And she desired him very, very much.

Cassie forced herself to drop her arms. She needed to make it animalistic again. "Dirk, if you're not inside me in twenty seconds, I'm getting up off this desk."

He made a sound between groaning and laughter. His hands framed her face and he met her gaze. "It will always be like this between us. It was always *us*," he said. Then he dipped his head and kissed her. A kiss she felt zap to every point of her body.

His hand returned to her panties, slipping inside to stroke her. Despite her earlier bravado of getting off her desk if he didn't get down to business soon, she was pretty much powerless to move. She only felt.

Felt the incredible sensations of pleasure as he gently caressed her, making her wetter. Felt the weight of him lift off of her as he unbuttoned his jeans and opened his fly. Felt the soft fabric of her panties brush against her clit as Dirk pushed them aside, in too much of a hurry to even drag them down her legs.

He teased her with the head of his erection until she arched and lifted her hips toward him. Then with a

moan, he sunk inside her, filling her finally. No slow seduction. No leisurely buildup. Just hot, desperate sex.

Cassie almost expected him to start pounding away. But…nothing. She opened her eyes to look at him. The muscles of his shoulders and neck corded under the strain of him holding back. She met his gaze, seeing the wonder in his eyes that must mirror her own.

Then he moved. He pulled gradually out of her body, only to slowly thrust back inside, sliding against every sensitive spot along the way.

She sucked in a breath and her eyes drifted shut again as pleasure made her inner muscles grip him hard. He drew himself from her slickness only to thrust back. Dirk did this over and over again. Building her pleasure. His lips and tongue caressed every part of her sensitized body. Her face, her neck, her breasts.

His fingers and hands stroked and teased her skin until every nerve ending in her body ached for his touch. When Dirk found her clitoris with the soft pad of his thumb, her hips bucked. She wrapped her legs around his waist, urging him on.

"Now, Dirk. Harder. Faster. Now."

He plunged into her. Her inner muscles clamped around him as wave after wave of pleasure took her over. Somewhere her brain registered that she was being loud, crying out in ecstasy. And she didn't care.

Dirk's muscles tensed beneath her fingertips and his thrusts became less controlled and more seeking. With a growl he exploded within her, triggering a second wave of pleasure.

After a few moments, Cassie caught her breath, but she wasn't ready to move yet. She felt too good. Her body too relaxed and complete. She didn't even care that her office desk was hard or that her stapler was poking her in the shoulder. She sunk her hands into Dirk's hair, loving the feel of the strands between her fingers.

He lifted his head, and their gazes met. Cassie was too content to try and mask any emotion that lingered in her eyes. Dirk lowered his lips and kissed her. A kiss so sweet and tender, full of renewal and promise her heart almost melted right there.

Maybe it was time to let go of the anger. He'd hurt her in the past, sure, but looking back, it wasn't unreasonable to have uncertainties. After all, it had only been the two of them for so long.

To be fair, she would ask any couple going through her premarriage counseling if they were still curious about other singles. If the answer was yes, she'd tell them to reexamine their commitment.

Had she expected Dirk to be too perfect?

He settled beside her, staring down into her eyes, as he gently brushed a few wayward curls from her face. So much for the sophisticated knot on the top of her head.

A sexy grin was at his lips. "Told you I was better at it."

If Dirk had stood up and poured a cold cup of water over her head, it wouldn't have been as jarring as the words he'd just said. If he'd slipped on heels and pranced around singing Prince she wouldn't have been more surprised.

Had he been so insulted when she'd told him she'd faked her orgasms that he'd gone on some mission to give her one? Had she mistaken hot, I-have-to-have-you-let's-do-it-on-your-desk sex for some sort of male, ego-motivated quest?

Every feel-good, great-sex induced endorphin ground to a halt. Replaced by cold denial.

Cassie struggled out of his arms.

"You can leave now," she said, glaring at the back of his head.

Dirk raised his head, his eyes still heavy with desire. "What?" he asked, sounding confused.

She swallowed over the tightness in her throat, trying to tug her shirt out from under his big arm. "I said it's time for you to go. I want you to leave."

"I thought maybe we could grab something to ea—"

"No."

His eyes narrowed, and his body tensed above her. "What are you saying? You're not hungry or you don't want to eat with me?"

"I'm saying I don't want to eat with you. This was a mistake."

"You're telling me this was a mistake when I'm still inside you?" he asked, his voice incredulous.

Cassie scrubbed her hand down her face. "Every-thing with you is a mistake, Dirk. I can't believe I'm here like this with you. I wrote a book about making better mistakes, and yet here I am again, repeating old ones."

Dirk lifted from her. No longer joined. His expres-sion grim. "That's pretty harsh. Did it make you feel

better to say that? To be the one to hurt me? Because I know I was the one to hurt you last time, and I'm sorry."

"Yeah, it felt good. You proved your point, and now you can go."

Dirk pushed himself off the table, his brows together in confusion. "Proved my point? What are you talking— Wait a minute. I know," he said as he snapped his fingers. "You think this was because I was riled over what you said. About me not giving you an orgasm."

"Exactly." Danni shoved her arm in the sleeve of her blouse. The wrinkles would be permanent; they'd screwed on top of it. She wouldn't call it anything else.

Dirk sighed heavily as he hauled his pants up into place. "Okay, poor choice of words. Just chalk it up under the *Dirk's Bad Moves* column. I'm sure that list is lengthy in your mind. Just so long as you know, I didn't mean it that way."

Cassie made a scoffing sound.

Dirk yanked the T-shirt over his head, his gaze meeting hers. Sadness tinged the blue of his eyes. "You have no intention of ever seeing me as anything other than the bad guy?"

She made a frustrated noise. "Because you are the bad guy."

"I'm not buying that. I've read your book, Cassie. You talk about communication, commitment, understanding. You cut everyone else in the world a break, but you can never give me any slack. I messed up. I made a mistake. You do that sometimes when you're twenty. If it's any consolation, I've regretted it ever since."

Cassie sucked in a breath, her heart beating faster. She did *not* want to hear this. Not now. She crossed her arms against her chest.

He met her eyes, his gaze direct and probing. "I love you, Cassie. I always will. Even knowing you think I'm lower than something stuck to the bottom of your shoe, I still want to spend the rest of my life with you. But I won't beat my head against the wall. I've done some form of that ever since college. You wouldn't take my calls. Never let me talk to you." He made a bitter sounding laugh. "Here I thought we were finally making progress."

Her throat tightened and she felt tears prick the back of her eyes.

Dirk pulled out his wallet, tossing his card on her desk. "That has my cell phone on it. Call me when you want to listen."

Then he stepped around her, careful not to touch her. She heard the outer door shut and she slumped into her chair. Cassie had just gotten everything she ever wanted from Dirk. He told her he was wrong. He admitted he still loved her. He asked to have her back.

Now should be the precise moment she should feel a rush of closure. That's what she'd wanted also, right? Satisfaction and closure?

Cassie fingered Dirk's card. Hating him worked. It felt right. Didn't it? She'd wrapped those strong emotions around her like a protective blanket. *Protection from what? Or whom?*

That she didn't want to think about.

Usually she'd be the first person to explain the importance of examining one's feelings. Owning the emotions. Release Not Retain was a chapter from her book.

But then usually her body still wasn't shaky from the most intense orgasm she'd ever had in her life. Uh-huh, avoidance looked pretty tempting right now.

13

DANNI GLANCED UP from her notes on legal termi-
nology. She couldn't concentrate. She'd woken this
morning with such a sense of foreboding it made her
nauseous. It wasn't Eric. He'd left her earlier this
morning with a sweet passionate kiss. She could sum
up her nervousness with one word.

Dad. That's when this gut-level anxiety first started.
But last night in Eric's arms she'd pushed aside the
strange apprehensive feelings. Now, however, in the
morning's bright sunlight, she couldn't ignore the
unease settling inside her.

Pushing away her textbook, she replayed conversations from the night before in her mind. Still, other
things seemed not quite right. With Eric?

Oh, he did and said all the right things, but there was
an aloofness about him. Almost a lack of real emotional involvement on his part. Except in bed. Never
there. Between the sheets he was fire.

Danni wrapped the blanket around her tighter.
Come to think of it, everything about Eric presented
an air of reservation. Oh, she'd seen hot fire and
passion in his eyes when they kissed. Loved the idea

of making this uptight corporate man lose control, but other than in bed, there felt like a disconnect between his words and his body language.

The expression in Eric's eyes never really matched his words. She'd spot a pulse pounding at his temple or his muscles going tight even in their most ordinary moments. Flynns were adept at dissecting the subtleties of nonverbal behavior. Except she'd missed so much. Why was that?

Because she only saw what she wanted to see?

Shaking her head, Danni padded to the bathroom. She was being ridiculous. This was regular Flynn behavior. Always questioning. Normal didn't sit well with her. That's why she had this strange feeling. Why she had the need to dissect his every action.

She turned on the spigot of the shower and stepped beneath the spray. The cold water jolted her back to reality. Eric was amazing. She loved him. She wasn't about to let her father start worming any doubts into her mind.

The water turned hot, and Danni adjusted the temperature. Sometime between soaping her body and rinsing her hair of conditioner, the thought that maybe she *should* check out Eric on the Internet entered her mind. What could it hurt?

She hadn't before because it seemed to be the opposite of her newfound ability to trust. Now it just seemed reckless.

After drying off, she slipped into a pair of lightweight pink shorts and one of the casino T-shirts. She

put her hair in a ponytail, and was ready to recon. First stop—the business center of the hotel.

Her fingers grew shaky after she swiped her keycard to enter the office services area, but she pulled out a chair and sat before a computer with resolve. Danni clicked for the search engine and typed in Eric's name.

A respectable amount of hits. She sighed in relief. Everything looked normal. She clicked on the first entry. Nope. Wrong Eric. Second and third Eric Reynolds were also for the wrong man—wrong age. Why couldn't she have fallen in love with a man whose last name was Unterseher?

Finally she found something, and her tension lessened once more as she reviewed the contents. Everything Eric had ever mentioned about himself, which was precious little, fit the record on the Internet. In fact, this entry was a press release from the casino announcing his hire. She found another site that mentioned him. That fit, too. Not giving her any additional information.

Okay, so he was a very private man.

With a smile, she logged off and made her way to the bank of elevators in the busy lobby. She stepped into the first open lift ready to shove these doubts right out of her mind. But…

Her smile faded. If everything fit, then what was wrong? She leaned against the elevator wall and watched the numbers ascend. There was *so little* information about him, when everyone left a trace. No one was that private. The tiny blurb she read downstairs felt

almost too convenient. The elevator doors opened, and she stepped out, deep in thought.

Come to think of it, a lot of things felt too convenient. Her mind slipped to their first meeting, and her stomach tensed. The hotel did everything for Eric. They had laundry facilities. He'd even suggested she use them. Why then had he been at *her* Laundromat? No one used that laundry on a Wednesday afternoon.

No one unless they were looking to meet someone. The dryer sheet flashed in her mind. He even arrived armed with a ready excuse to talk to her. Not once had she seen that laundry basket he'd used for his clothes tucked somewhere in the suite.

She shook her head as she keyed into the room. No. She was blowing this out of proportion. Damn her father. He always ruined everything. Eric was perfect. He'd never been shocked by her past. He knew exactly what to say. How to make her feel. She trusted him completely.

But was that by design? How did the man know exactly what to say to make her trust him? She barely trusted anyone. Been raised not to. And yet Eric had managed to sidestep every red flag her mind would naturally raise.

She smelled a rat.

Her palms began to sweat, and she grew sick to her stomach. Like a shot, Danni began to snoop. Why she hadn't before was beyond her. Nothing under the bed, under the drawers or between the mattresses. She scanned the room looking for the perfect place to hide something. Anything.

The safe the hotel provided in the closet was too obvious. Personal. It wouldn't be in the room. It was too easy for her to accidentally stumble onto something.

His office. He spent a lot of time there, and he'd never invited her back, instead steering her toward a conference room whenever they discussed hotel business.

She thought of that first time he'd invited her to his office. He'd left her alone. Files left within an easy glance, or even a casual perusal of the room. It all made sense now.

He'd left her there alone.

For a long time.

With vital security information within her reach.

It had been a setup. It had all been a setup.

But still, a burning hope gave him the benefit of the doubt. *She had to know.*

Danni flew out of the suite and to the elevators, jamming the button over and over until the green down arrow lit. She stepped inside, coaching herself to look calm. Nonchalant. On the casino floor, she crept along the outskirts so as not to run directly into Eric.

But he had a meeting at the gaming commission. He wouldn't even be around the casino today. She smiled and walked directly to the side where the administrative offices were located. A U-shaped reception desk provided her first block. Eric's office was right around the corner, but she had to get past that receptionist first. She'd met the woman plenty of times, so her presence wouldn't come as a surprise.

Her opportunity came in the form of a phone call.

The receptionist lifted the receiver to her ear, and that's when Danni made her move. She rounded the corner as if in a hurry, and opened her mouth to speak.

The woman lifted a stressed brow as she approached. Yeah, she hated working multi-line phones, too.

"It's okay," Danni mouthed with a wink, and pointed to her watch as if she had an appointment with someone.

The woman guarding the desk gave her a relieved wave.

On swift legs, Danni flew down the corridor before the woman rang off and decided to announce her arrival. Half the success of the con was confidence and taking advantage of an opportunity.

Danni jimmied the door to Eric's office and slipped inside. That was the thing about security people. They never thought they'd be ripped off, so usually used the lowest form of protection on the job. *Suckers.*

She'd dash off a note to Eric suggesting coded locks if her suspicions turned out to be true. Just to let him know how easy he was to break.

She scanned the room. His office was nothing but a closed-off storage room. Still virtually nothing on the walls. No warmth. No clues to the man.

She started with his vertical hanging files. Nothing out of the ordinary. Nothing popped out at her from his pencil drawer, bookcase or credenza. The only thing in his large desk drawer was his gym bag, and she closed the drawer quietly so no one would hear.

Danni sat on the back of her heels, giving the room a second look. It was here. The proof of whatever was up with Eric lay in this room. She knew it. He was just too good. Too perfect. Too practiced to be true.

Why would someone store their gym bag in a desk drawer?

No one with nothing to hide, that's who. She yanked the drawer open again, grabbed the bag and dropped it onto the floor. With determined fingers she slammed the zipper open.

He'd stuffed the top with smelly socks. Amateur. That was one of the oldest tricks in the book.

Under the sweatpants and dirty T-shirt she found a locked box. Again, why would any normal man keep a lockbox in his workout bag?

That was her answer.

Danni examined the lock, then gave a bitter laugh. Now this was almost downright insulting. She could pick that lock in about five minutes. Less time if she had the proper tools. She sneered. He must have thought he had her so besotted. Anger filled her.

Exactly three minutes later, the lock popped free in her hand. She had total rein to snoop. Instead, she took a deep breath and stared at the unopened lockbox on the carpet at her knees. This was her last chance. Her last moment of true trust.

She could still relock the lock, return everything to its natural hiding place and never think of this again. If she opened that box, and it turned out she was wrong about Eric, her actions right now would taint every-

thing. She'd have to tell him what she'd done. That's what honest—normal—people did.

Everything they'd done together she now viewed differently. Danni closed her eyes at the memory of them roasting marshmallows. She'd never done anything so simple and fun. He'd planned the most romantic date.

Planning. That was the key.

Danni opened her eyes. Determined. Everything on his part seemed a touch planned. From the timing of his calls to the drawing out of their passion until she couldn't think straight she wanted him so badly.

With a frustrated cry she lifted the lid of the lockbox, and gasped when she saw a gun. She sucked in a breath. So he had a gun. He was head of security. It would be weird if he didn't have a gun. That might explain why he'd hidden it.

Still, she continued her search. Among a few file folders, a box of ammunition nestled along a leather card holder. The kind used to house an official badge. She grasped it, holding her breath and hoping she wouldn't see what she knew she would. Danni flipped the holder open.

It was all there. Crest. Badge number. His picture. And the words Federal Agent. She allowed one tear to slip past her lashes. One heartbreaking swallow of sadness.

Then she closed Eric's badge holder, replaced everything in the box and sealed it. She returned everything in the room to exactly how she'd found it, and

carefully slipped out of the room. She had to get somewhere. Someplace to think.

Luckily Eric hadn't returned to the casino yet, so she made her way to the parking lot. She reached for her cell phone to call Cassie. Wait, what if they had it bugged? Her car on some sort of geo-positioning satellite?

All right, now she was being paranoid. But still, she returned to the front door of the casino and slid into one of the waiting taxis. She'd go to some restaurant she'd never been to before, then call Cassie. Her fingers shook as she dialed the number.

Thirty minutes later, Cassie joined Danni at the diner around the corner from her office. Danni's initial shakes were over, and she'd already settled into a nice simmering anger.

Cassie looked worried and extremely distracted. "I'm glad you called, because I think I just made the biggest mistake of my life. Or the best. I can't decide."

Danni settled against her chair, anxious to hear Cassie's problems. Anything to put off facing her own. "I can't wait to hear this."

"I had sex with Dirk. Really quick. Really mistake-in-judgment kind of sex."

"Is this good or bad?"

Cassie sighed. "I don't know. The sex was terrific."

"Well, hey. That's good."

Cassie's expression grew tortured. "Danni, he told me he still loves me. In fact, he made it sound like he wants to be with me."

"What exactly did he say?" It had been her experience that women could dissect and overanalyze the most innocently man-made sentences and turn them into something that barely resembled their clear intention.

"That he wanted to be with me the rest of his life."

"That pretty much sounds like forever." Good for her. Nice to know you were actually wanted, rather than someone's mark. She swallowed back the sarcastic response, and took on Cassie's more familiar counselor role. "Is that what you want?"

"It was at one point. Now, I'm not so sure. I've wanted to hate him for so long, it's hard to give that up. I've never really stopped loving him." Cassie ripped the band holding her hair in place. "Ugh, how pathetic am I?"

"Join the club, because I'm just as pathetic. Eric is a federal agent. If that's really his name. I forgot to check after I saw the badge."

"What?" Cassie asked, her expression confused.

Danni sank her head into her hands. "Man, he played me against the wall. Drew me right into the casino and everything. I am such a sucker."

Cassie shook her head. "So he has a different job— what's the big deal?"

Danni looked over her shoulder. No one seemed to be skulking in the background, so she leaned forward. "Cassie, you've lived in Nevada all your life, right?" At Cassie's nod, Danni continued. "Then you'd be familiar with a big casino heist in Vegas."

Cassie gasped. "Not the one at the Western Nugget?"

Danni only nodded, still a touch paranoid about talking about this.

Her friend whistled. "That's the most famous casino theft ever. There's been nothing like it for years."

After the job, known as the Western Nugget heist, went down, things went bad. Her father warned her never to speak of it again. Not even to think about it. Daniel spoke of it in such vague terms, sometimes she wasn't even sure he was involved or only being cautious.

"I was surprised my father mentioned it to me."

Cassie's brows lifted, the perfect picture of curiosity. "Your dad was part of that? That money was never recovered. Or spent."

"I was never completely clear on that either. He might have played a role, he might not have… There were some pretty shady characters involved. Not the type of work my father was used to. Word on the street was that the ringleaders used a man who knew his way around a casino."

"This blows my mind. Even with knowing your family history all this time, I never suspected, never even thought that you might know something about it."

"They arrested me right after the heist for another con I was involved in, so some big score was the last thing I was thinking about. It wasn't until my father reminded me of it yesterday…well, he made some big hints. He still won't confirm. See, the people involved, some of them are dead. Like I said, pretty shady. He wouldn't want me involved."

"But your father's been out of jail for a while. Why hasn't he gone for it if he can?"

"From what I've gathered, the money's in a Swiss bank account."

"Why not transfer it here?"

Danni smiled. "Ah, there you go. Thinking like an honest person again. Transfers leave trails. With the new banking laws, almost every bank would not only refuse a confidential transfer, but more than likely report a request. No, if he's involved he'd have to go to Switzerland. And for that he needs cash."

"Well, then you have nothing to worry about. He won't be leaving the country anytime soon. He's broke and living in a halfway house."

Danni swallowed. "Except he's asked me to steal some dice from the casino."

"To do what exactly?" asked Cassie, her expression growing shrewd.

"He didn't say, but I expect it's to magnetize them. It will be easy enough to hide a magnet somewhere on him. He'd win at craps whenever he wanted."

"And pay for his ticket. Fake passport."

"Now you're thinking like my dad." Danni rubbed the bridge of her nose. "I told him no, of course. But then he started heaping on the guilt. It's a great tool of his."

"Danni, what on earth do you have to feel guilty about? The man led you into a life of crime. Not the other way around."

"Yes, but I was the one who got caught. Caught because I didn't follow the rules of the con he'd staged.

He could have left. Skipped town and never come back, but he didn't do that. He cut a deal with the DA. He went to prison while I just went to juvie. So in a way, I do owe him."

Cassie reached for Danni's hand and gave it a supportive squeeze. "Danni, he did what a father should have been doing all along. Protecting his child. You should never have been in that position in the first place. We've talked about this misplaced loyalty to him in the past."

Danni nodded, knowing what Cassie said was true. "Yes, but feelings are feelings no matter how irrational they are."

"Where does Eric come in?"

"Solving that Western Nugget heist has been a hobby for many a lawman. I've even seen segments re-creating the theft on those unsolved mystery type shows. I fell perfectly into Eric's hands. So trusting. So in love. I bet the jerk gave me such free access to the casino in the hopes that I'd do something illegal. Since my father had come to my rescue once before and acted the fall guy, the authorities probably thought he'd do so again. The DA has been out to get my dad ever since he cut that deal."

"Why?"

"Because my dad signed the deal with the DA before any hint of his involvement in the heist came to light. The prosecutor was bitter about his mistake. Even if Dad is a part of it, he leaves no trails. Only I do that," she said, feeling guilty again, and dumb. "Now Eric's using me to create a bargaining chip. I do

something wrong and Daddy comes to the rescue, again. Only this time, the price to keep me out of jail is to spill where the money is."

"Danni, surely not. Maybe he's retired? Maybe he *is* just a security chief?"

"And maybe it's only coincidence that I'm the daughter of one of the most sought-after thieves in Nevada. No. There are no coincidences. Only opportunities. You know who told me that? Eric. When I think of those dates we had…all that subtle pumping for information about my father. Man, I could punch myself for being such a dupe," she said, her hands flailing.

"I can't believe a federal agent would lie like that."

"Oh, it's perfectly legal. You know, I've heard of some real dirty cons in my life, but this takes the cake. He put the artist in con artist. He's a con heartist. The big lying liar." Okay, she was leaning on the hysterical side with the frantic arm action and over-the-top expressions. Danni took a calming breath.

"There's got to be a bright side to this. You haven't done anything wrong."

"I know," she said, her tone sarcastic. "If this works out and Eric solves the crime, I could be used in case studies when they train new agents." Danni groaned into her hands, the humiliation of it almost as painful to think of as Eric's duplicitous kisses. *The jerk.*

"Generations of Flynns are spinning in their graves."

"What are you going to do?"

"Warn my father, I guess. Although I should probably let him lie in the bed he's made. I can't believe

he would do this. Right before they shipped him off to prison, the police allowed us thirty minutes together. I made him promise, promise me the thieving life was over. He looked me straight in the eye and agreed. That's why he told me never to talk about that money."

"No doubt, the less you knew, the better."

"He said he had no intention of ever touching that stolen money, although not in so many words. It was all very cryptic."

"What are you going to do about Eric?"

Danni shrugged, way beyond bitter. "What about him? He'll be gone soon anyway. Once he realizes his long con is a bust. He never did carry much of an air of permanency. To tell you the truth, I'm a lot more interested in hearing about you and Dirk." Anything to keep her mind off the pathetic path her love life had taken.

"But Eric hurt you and you're suppressing the anger."

Cassie's brow wrinkled. Oh yeah, Danni thought, her friend was in full counsel mode. But Danni didn't need a diagnosis. She was pissed and heartbroken. Pissed.

"And so what if I am? Maybe I'm not like you, Cassie. I don't need to acknowledge and own every emotion I have. I wasn't paying attention. I dropped my guard and fell in love. He broke my heart, as I should have expected all along, and now it's time to move on. Case closed," she announced, her voice cracking.

Cassie tapped her finger against her chin. "Could the problem be that I was born a romantic and became a cynic? You were born a cynic and became a romantic?"

Danni nodded. "Either way, I think my transformation

sucks more. It's confirmation that I was stupid. Knew that I could get stupid, and still went with stupid anyway."

Cassie raised her gaze. "Was stupid worth it?"

An image of Eric's, if that were even his real name, face pummeled at her. Everything about him was gorgeous. Everything about him appealed to her, made sense to her. Past losers only borrowed money, didn't pay it back and split. Eric, with his seductive touches, stole way more than money.

No. Stupid wasn't worth it. Stupid brought a physical ache. But Danni could spot Cassie's intentions from a mile away. This was her means of leading Danni into some discussion about emotional growth, and wasn't the pain a small price to pay because it led to more self-discovery crap. Blah, blah, blah.

Well, Danni already knew she liked her emotions suppressed.

Cassie didn't. Danni gave her friend another once-over. Sure, she appeared sad, but she didn't have the I'm-going-to-bash-his-new-plasma-screen-TV-with-a-baseball-bat look. Like how Danni felt. Cassie didn't seem angry enough to have been truly hurt by the man she loved.

"Cassie, about Dirk. Couldn't it be that when he was young and stupid, he did a young and stupid thing? He says he loves you. Has always loved you."

"Pfttt."

"He said he regretted it, right? He made a mistake— how long are you going to make him suffer for it?"

"Forever works."

"Come on, you can't pretend to be the cynic with me. You don't have the street cred."

Cassie met her eyes. Utter vulnerability passed across her face. "I loved him. He broke my heart."

The simple words, so from the gut, kicked her in the heart. Yeah. She loved him. He broke her heart. Just like Eric. But Dirk wasn't Eric.

"He did those things years ago. He's admitted he was wrong."

"I don't know if I can trust him."

Aha. So she'd thought about it. That was pretty telling. "How about you just treat him really bad?"

Cassie's gaze lowered. "Already done that."

"Then, maybe you're up against the real thing."

"What if this isn't? I let him in and he ruins my heart once more."

"Then you embrace the cynicism again. But do you never really want to know? To go the whole rest of your life and not find out if you could have had that happy ending with Dirk?"

CASSIE TALKED WITH DANNI until the daylight faded and the stars began to shine in the sky. Cassie could have talked longer, but she had to go back and tidy up her desk and set the alarms.

She skirted around a couple of skateboarders and almost ran into a man juggling takeout. Danni's direct question from earlier still had her thinking. Her best friend had stared her square in the eye and asked her point

blank, "Cassie, don't you think the person you need to be saying these things to is Dirk? Release, not retain."

She hated it when her best friend threw her own words in her face. And that was the heart of the problem. If she were her client, she'd be telling herself to forgive. Give Dirk a try and find a new person to hate. It had been her experience that men didn't open up and admit they were wrong very often.

Her heart warmed and she smiled at the memory of him confessing he still loved her. Always would.

Cassie unlocked the front door and stepped inside. Heather had already straightened up the outer office so all that was left for Cassie to do was sort through her case files and power off her computer. She tried to avoid lingering at her desk. A desk that showed no evidence of the lovemaking earlier.

Except for Dirk's card with his cell number on it. She fingered the card for a moment. He hadn't left her office under the best of circumstances. She hadn't made him leave that way.

Decision made, she dialed his number. He answered on the first ring.

"This isn't the way to start off a relationship."

Dirk made a noise that sounded a cross between a laugh and a sigh of relief. "I'll start it anyway you'll let me."

Her heart jump-started at the sexy timbre in his voice. Yes, this was the right decision. Probably. "You need to start off with a few explanations first. Then I'll decide."

"Okay."

"How do I know you won't realize you need time to figure us out again?"

"Cassie, I have been dating over the last ten years, just like you. But there's a reason why I'm still alone. I want you. Anyone else I would just be settling for. Now you need to decide. You going to keep punishing me for some stupid thing I did when I was twenty?"

"You hurt me. You made me question myself. Made me ask what was so wrong with me that you didn't want me to be yours anymore."

"I know, and I'm sorry. Believe me when I say that I've tortured myself for making such a mistake." The regret and pain in his voice made tears prick the back of her eyes.

"I just don't know if it's as much torture as I think you deserve."

"But if it makes you feel any better I'll drive to Reno right now and you can smack my ass like you promised."

She laughed, feeling lighter. That didn't sound half bad. She shook her head to release the image of his backside. "I'm still angry."

"Yes, but are your nipples hard?" he asked, his voice rich, deep and sexy.

She gasped at his shocking question.

I made the biggest mistake of my life.

The outrageous provocateur and the sensitive man who apologized for hurting her were one and the same. He was a complex person who made mistakes.

Could she trust him with her heart again?

She had to be grinning like a fool. She just had to

be. Dirk had found a way to slip beneath her defenses with his open blend of simple honesty and humor.

"Maybe they're a little hard." She shook her head. "This is not a healthy relationship," she told him, her voice rising. "Do you hear that noise?"

"What?"

"That tone in my voice? I am becoming shrill."

"I love you, Cassie. I've never told another person that in my life."

She swallowed around the lump in her throat. She wasn't ready to hear this yet. "You know, I didn't even like you at first. I thought you were icky."

"Icky? Well, I thought all girls were icky until you came along and blew me away," he said, laughing. Then his voice grew serious. "Say the word, Cassie. Say the word and I'll drive up to Reno right now."

"Soon," she promised.

14

ALL THE PIECES OF the plan were falling into place. Danni trusted him, he'd given her controlled access to the casino and her father had made an appearance.

Wouldn't be long now.

He grew edgy. In his past undercover work, this would be the precise moment when he knew all the careful planning and hours of research would not be wasted. He'd make the bust and know with satisfaction justice had been served.

Then why was he not feeling those same things now?

This was it. This was what he'd been waiting for. What all the members of the task force had been waiting for, and here he was almost wishing this sting would fail.

It was the first mistake in undercover work, and he'd made it. He'd become involved. Somehow, some way he'd grown to care about Danni and what happened to her. He'd even had thoughts about their future. Together.

All that was bust though, if he didn't get control over what was happening between him and Danni.

His walkie-talkie clicked. "You're not going to believe this, boss, but Gold Standard is at reception. He wants to make an appointment."

Sweet satisfaction filled Eric, and he realized with relief that he was still the lawman. He was the person he thought himself to be. In fact, he'd been looking at this the wrong way: the sooner Danni's father made his move, the sooner Eric could move on. *They* could move on. All this time everyone on the task force assumed she'd aid her father. But none of them knew this new Danni Flynn. The woman trying to make right. The woman who looked Eric in the eyes and told him he could trust her.

"Book the GS for tonight. Danni has class. You know the drill. Have everything in place."

Early in the mission, the members of his team had begun referring to Daniel Flynn as Gold Standard, since he'd allegedly set the benchmark for which all other casino robberies would be compared.

"Done. Looks like he's not involving Danni," Eric's second in command said. Did he denote a touch of relief in the man's voice? Eric wouldn't doubt it. He smiled as he scanned the casino for her. It appeared Danni had convinced not just him that she deserved a second chance.

The team had given Danni a moniker, too. Gold Magnet. Didn't fit anymore, though. Now everyone pretty much called her Danni.

Eric switched channels on his walkie-talkie. "Where is Danni?" he asked the staff in the casino's security control room. Was Danni where she could observe her father?

"I don't see her," the man on duty said. The eye in

the sky cameras throughout the casino would have picked her up if she'd been on the floor. She wasn't scheduled to work right now, but it was his job to know where she was at all times.

He didn't panic. Eric never panicked. A cool head and simple logic made him a natural to work under-cover. His gut instinct kept him from making mistakes. And now something didn't feel right.

Eric nearly sprinted to the elevator. He had to see, reassure himself that Danni was there in the suite, rather than doing some potentially criminal act on behalf of her father.

But the room was empty. And his suspicions were piqued. He called her apartment, only got her answer-ing machine. He left a message, shooting for concerned boyfriend rather than apprehensive undercover lawman.

DANNI UNLOCKED her apartment, and musty air hit her. She hadn't been home in a couple of days, preferring to stay with Eric in his suite. Idiot.

Now it felt good to be in familiar surroundings. She could trust her old-fashioned couch. Her faith wouldn't be misplaced in the futon she'd bought new at the supercenter. And she had absolute confidence in the two mismatched chairs in the kitchen.

She didn't reside in a lavish space in a beautiful hotel. Though her cheap apartment with the drooping blinds and faded carpet was at least no Eric-created illusion. Rubbing her temples, Danni flattened her back against the wall.

She'd gotten a headache from grinding her back teeth in anger. Danni welcomed the anger. It was a lot easier to deal with than the pain, and the thought of Eric's sexy eyes and promising smile. And lying mouth. *Jerk.* May he'd get poked by the pin of his badge and his tetanus wouldn't be up-to-date.

First things first. She had to warn her dad the feds were on to him. Maybe the threat of another brush with the law would scare him straight. Although if his promises to his own daughter and several years in prison hadn't done the trick, she wasn't sure this would.

The message light on her machine was blinking twice. Her heartbeat quickened, because she knew one of the messages had to be from Eric. She'd turned off her cell phone. Did the agent need to contact his prey? She pressed the message button.

"I didn't see you on the floor during my rounds. I just wanted to make sure you were okay." That deep voice of his didn't match her new Eric Reynolds image.

"Yeah, as if you care," she said. Danni closed her eyes and bit on her bottom lip as the hurt of hearing Eric's insincere, deceitful, two-faced…

Danni took a deep breath. She was dancing too close to the hysteria line again. She bit her lip hard, and for one moment she let the hurt she'd held tight really flow through her. Eric. He had a job to do, she could understand that on some level. Why'd he have to do it like that? Why'd he have to make her love him? Why'd he make her crave things she knew she had no business yearning for in the first place.

He dangled the one thing she hungered for above everything else. Love. Respectful, mutual, passionate love. It was a need she hadn't even realized she had until Eric awoke it in her. He was clearly very good at his job. He'd studied her well.

Come to think of it, Eric's whole message was annoying. He never just asked something along the lines of, "Would you like to have dinner with me?" It was always "Let's do this" or "Come with me to this" as if her agreement was implied. Although it had been.

Ugh. No more take-charge, alpha-type men for her in the future. Losers from now on all the way. There was something a girl could trust about a man she had low expectations of.

Danni had been so excited about Eric at first. So determined to change her dating habits. How much better off would she have been if she'd stuck to her old habits?

A lot. She deleted his message with a jab from her finger.

The next message was from her dad. "Danni-bear, don't worry about that thing we talked about earlier." Danni sighed in relief. "I've worked things out on my own. I'm meeting with your boyfriend tonight."

Danni sucked in a breath in panic. Eric moved fast. Had she left a trace that she'd been snooping? Had her hasty exit with no explanation tipped him off? She broke out in a sweat and her hands grew shaky again.

Grab and go. That was the Flynn plan of action whenever a con went bust. She picked up the receiver

and dialed her father's number at the halfway house. He needed to go, and forget the grabbing.

No answer. Danni grunted in frustration.

She must tip off her father before Eric got to him. Somehow she must distract the lying jerk long enough, restrain him somehow…

Tie him up.

Her eyes widened. Of course. It was perfect and he wouldn't suspect a thing. Despite the utter anger she felt toward him, her body still reacted as she remembered how he'd let her tie him up and do whatever she wanted to with him, and how he enjoyed it.

He'd trusted her then.

No, it was just more tactic he'd used to get her to trust him.

Wait a minute. The man had rocked her world. Why shouldn't he do it one more time? The lower-than-pond-scum liar owed her at least an amazing farewell orgasm before she told him goodbye. And if a few of his law enforcement buddies happened to stumble into his suite and find him naked and tied up…

A smile broke across her face. Oh, yeah, she'd leave him like that in the room for anyone to find. Or she could phone in a tip to some hotline. She almost laughed out loud at the image of news cameras bursting into his room trying to catch a crime in progress for the evening news. The feds could add that little detail to their case study.

In a rush now, Danni grabbed her duffel bag and began stuffing it with rope and duct tape. She tossed in

a few silky scarves to throw him off the scent. It was time to execute a seduction of her own this time. The Danni Flynn version of the romance con on Eric Reynolds.

Her plan was simple. Draw him away from the floor, up to his room. She'd put *him* on the send for a change. Do him, then do the deed. He wouldn't be forgetting the convincer she planned to give him for a long time.

ERIC GRIPPED Danni by the hips, his cock already to a painful point. How many times had she been in his arms in this elevator? And here they were again on the way to his suite, when he'd had every intention of slowing things down between them.

He was crazy. He was crazy. He was crazy. But then Danni made him crazy. A simple assignment. A simple case of laying out the bait, and Eric would have the means to get the money and the crook all at the same time. His career would skyrocket.

So why did he feel guilty? He rubbed his jaw in frustration.

The guilt came about the time he fell in love with Danni. Eric could pinpoint the precise moment when it happened. When he began to think of Danni as a woman he wanted to be connected to, rather than as an asset to his case. When she snuggled against his chest as they sat beneath the stars and she told him of the little girl she'd once been. The little girl who'd stand next to a mother in a store, pretending for a moment that she was hers.

Foolishly, he'd thought her father might not take the bait. That Daniel really had turned a new leaf. That the investigation could take another turn, and he could take another turn in his relationship with Danni, too.

Then her father made his move. Didn't the bastard know what he'd done to his own daughter? Danni Flynn craved a life of normal things.

Before he'd met Danni, fell in love with her, he'd looked forward to catching her father. Now Eric faced Daniel's next move with dread. How did you tell the woman you've been sleeping with that you'd started the whole thing to slam her father back into jail?

"Danni," he began. He should do it now, despite the white-hot desire she stirred in him.

Her eyes turned to slits. She was absolutely beautiful. He could spend all day in bed looking at this blond goddess. She placed her finger against his lips. "Shut up and kiss me," she told him. Then she moved her finger and replaced it with her mouth.

Her honey taste was addictive. Nothing smelled better than her hair, and all he could think of was burying himself in her.

There was a determination about her tonight. Almost ruthless. This was new from her. It excited him. But then everything Danni did excited him.

It hurt like hell to break apart from her as the ding of the elevator sounded. His breath came in pants.

He should try again to tell her. He really should.

Then her eyes found his. "I want you right now," she said in a tone that made his cock throb.

He'd tell her after.

How many times had he rushed her to his room? That first time they hadn't even gotten their clothes off. Almost didn't the second. She was passion and temptation, and tonight she was intriguing aggression.

He fished for his keycard. "I hated finding this bed empty today," he said after he opened the door.

"Don't talk," she said as she tugged his shirt from the waistband of his pants.

Eric couldn't get enough of this woman, hauling her against him. His fingers made quick work of the buttons of her blouse, only to groan when he saw the sexy black bra she wore.

"You're so naughty. It turns me on so much."

Danni pulled away from him, walking backwards to the bed as she lowered the straps of her bra. There was a gleam in her eye that made him think of stroking every inch of her breasts. "Then come get me," she said, her voice carnal, filled with wicked promise.

He glanced toward the clock. He was to meet with her father in less than two hours to set the final plan in action. Eric was to play the classic dupe to her father's consummate con artist.

Yet, he still felt nagging guilt.

If her father took the bait, then that was that. Daniel Flynn was a grown man who could always walk away. Whatever her old man decided, it had nothing to do with them. Eric wouldn't let it. He'd comfort her. He'd hold her. He'd…love her.

Yes, he'd love her. He loved her.

She'd be hurt when she learned of his involvement. There was no getting around that, but he had the rest of his life to make it up to her. And he'd hire her father a good lawyer. Something he'd never thought he'd do.

Eric turned his head to face her. Drink in her beautiful body. This wasn't about Daniel Flynn. This heat. This passion was about them. Nothing else.

Right now he wanted her out of that bra, those sexy low-ride panties and up on the bed. He stalked toward her, his fingers already circling her back for the clasp. With a quick snap, it fell to the floor and her luscious breasts were for his eyes only.

She sucked in a breath when his tongue found her nipple, growing tighter within his mouth. He loved hearing her gasp and moan. Loved the feeling of her body shivering at his touch. She was perfect.

Eric ran his hands down her waist. He lifted her into his arms and onto the bed. Followed her down to the mattress.

Danni seemed tense tonight, preoccupied. Her gaze wouldn't quite meet his, and she'd flinched slightly when he first returned her caresses. He had been taking her away from her studies. He knew what to do to make her relax.

He kissed a path down her rib cage and over the sweet softness of her belly. Her muscles dipped and contracted under the touch of his tongue. Her silky black panties barely covered anything, and served only to tease and tempt him further. He nipped at the edge with his teeth, drawing them down her hips until she

lay naked before him. Eric gently gripped her knees, pushing them apart with his shoulders.

He found her wet and he couldn't wait to drive her crazy, feel her hips arch against his lips.

Danni cried out as he tasted her. Her fingers dug into his shoulders. He loved giving her pleasure. Wanted to keep giving her more.

Danni's grip on his back tightened as she tried to pull him upwards. "I don't…it's too much…"

Her words trailed off, but he knew what she needed. It took a lot for this woman to trust. Right now before him, she was too open, too exposed. She wanted sex to be a game, a power play. He could work within those confines. Hell, he loved working in those confines. Soon, she'd trust him fully.

He lifted from her body, and Danni towed him upward until he braced himself above her body. She closed her eyes rather than meet his gaze, but her beautiful face was a study in concentration.

Hooking her leg around his hips, she tugged him toward her, sending his erection into direct contact with her slick heat. He paused for a moment, getting the condom in place. Then he thrust inside her, closing his eyes with how good she felt surrounding him.

She met his thrusts, running her fingers along his hips. Making him drive harder, deeper when her hands teased his skin.

"Danni, you're so incredible," he breathed into her ear. He'd never come across a woman as strong and determined as she was. His fingers found her nipple and

he gently stroked her. He'd never get enough of stroking this woman. And hearing her sigh in response.

She tensed below him, and he stilled. "Something wrong?" he asked.

"Everything's...wonderful," she said, keeping her eyes closed.

But he knew something wasn't quite right. Although they were new lovers, he'd already memorized every spot to caress that made her gasp. He longed to have her moan as she came apart in his arms.

"You feel so good, Danni," he told her, his voice sounding ragged.

She sighed and made a moan deep in her throat. Now that was more like it. He stroked inside her harder now, wanting to send her over the edge. Suddenly she gripped his strong shoulders and pushed him away, their bodies stayed joined.

"I have a game I want to play," she said, her voice a sexy temptation.

"You and your games."

"I want to tie you up and then do naughty things to your body."

Now? She wanted to stop and play a game now? "Next time," he promised.

She shook her head and smiled. Pure provocative invitation. He'd probably agree to anything right now.

"No, it will be more fun this way. Our bodies will ache for completion, but we won't let them have it until we turn up the heat even more. It will be almost tantric."

Eric made a noise deep in his throat at the torturous

image she'd planted in his head. "I can never say no to you." He wrapped her in his arms, breathing deep of her flowery feminine scent.

But his woman wanted to play a game. Reluctantly he rolled so she straddled him. She cried out above him as this new position drove him deeper into her, and he groaned.

"I'm all yours," he said, biting back his frustration.

"You just bet you will be."

"What?" he asked, opening his eyes to a great view of her breasts.

Danni shook her head and smiled. "Nothing. I have the rope in my bag," she told him.

His gaze moved upward and he met her eyes. A glint glowed there, and her hair was a wild mane. His woman was a hellcat. He was so damn lucky. "You came prepared."

That mysterious smile of hers only made him want her more.

Eric groaned again as she pulled away from his erection. He couldn't take his eyes off her amazing body as she took way too long to reach her bag. He needed her in bed. Now.

She tossed her bag on the bedside table, then returned to him in a slow stride that made her hips sway. Everything about her at this moment was about the seduction, and his response was primal.

Bringing out a rope, Danni became all business. And that rope was all business. Thick with large knots. A small trickle of unease ran down his back. This was

definitely not the tie from before. "You're serious. I expected a scarf or something."

She winked then reached over and drew out the kind of fluffy scarves he'd anticipated. "The scarf I'll put against your skin. That way you won't get chafed. Wouldn't want you showing up to work with burn marks. Trust me," she said.

At this point, she could probably convince him burn marks wouldn't be so bad. Eric lifted his hand.

Danni pressed a kiss on the skin of his wrist, sending a shock down his arm. The scarf slid into place. Using the rope, she secured his arm to the bedpost. Every nerve ending ached as she secured his other arm and both legs. Every graze of her skin against his, every accidental touch ratcheted up his need for her.

Danni's expression grew guarded as she stroked the hair away from his face. She trailed her finger along his strong cheekbone and jaw, before she got to his lips. Eric sucked in a breath as she leisurely traced a path over his chest and abs.

Danni bent over, and traced his bottom lip with her tongue. She tasted like wine and sexy woman. She tasted like his.

Danni kissed him hard. He also tasted something sad and…bitter on her lips. She touched him as if she were trying to commit the feel of him to her memory. When only the sounds of their ragged breathing filled the bedroom of his suite, she scrambled off the bed.

He lifted his head, seeing her sexy backside as she

searched for something on the floor "What are you doing?" he asked.

Danni's head shot up, her expression concerned. All traces of desire gone. He watched her grab her jeans. "What do you think I'm doing? I'm getting dressed."

"What?" He managed to sit up higher, watch her slip into her bra.

"I'm leaving."

"What the hell…? Danni, this isn't funny." Eric tugged hard at his bonds.

She finally met his gaze. No trace of the trust or the love he'd spotted in her eyes yesterday. Just hurt and anger. And cold calculation.

"I'm not meaning it to be a joke."

Eric began to strain against the rope, pulling with his arms. Something was very, very wrong here.

"I wasn't lying about being a Scout," she said. "I really do know how to make good knots. Don't worry, despite the Do Not Disturb sign I placed on the knob, I'll call room service to come get you. After a few hours. That should give you plenty of time to reflect on your crimes."

He was way past irritation now. Anger suffused his body, chasing away the last vestiges of desire. He made the mistake of meeting her eyes again. Apparently he'd made a lot of mistakes. Apparently something she witnessed in his eyes made her nervous. He saw her blanch and take a step back. He didn't need a woman with punishment on her mind nervous. She reached for a roll of duct tape as she made her way back to the bed. "What are you planning to do with that?"

Danni held her shoulders stiff with each step toward him. Good. He could still talk to her. Try to calm her down. Get out of these damn ropes.

Once at the bed, Danni unrolled a long strip of tape.

"Danni, stop this. You're making a mistake," he pleaded.

Danni shook her head. "I doubt it. You picked the wrong mark, ace."

"Mark? What are you talking about?"

"Someone has to save my father."

Alarm raced through his body. She knew. Or at least she thought she knew. He shoved against the rope, he had to make her understand.

Then he saw the hurt in her eyes. He was such an idiot. He should have gone with his instinct to tell her the truth when they first entered this room. The last thing he'd wanted to do was to hurt her.

"Danni, whatever it is you think you know, you're wrong. Let me expl—"

"Save your explanation. It will all just be more lies." She held the tape only inches from his mouth.

He searched for something, anything that could help him. And he spotted the loosened knot around his left wrist. He stopped his struggles. He didn't want to give her any reason to examine his bonds again.

But he felt a fear like he'd never felt before in his life. Knew in his gut something was about to go down with Daniel Flynn. The man he'd spotted following Daniel Flynn two days ago was the type of criminal best left locked behind bars. Not near Danni.

He'd kept her safe by keeping her by his side. But now she could walk into something dangerous, something he did not want her involved in if she left here and tried to warn her father.

He'd trail her. See where she led him. Then take her to safety. Force her if he had to. First, he'd have to suffer her sticking tape over his mouth. He made a mental note never to get Danni mad at him after this.

She loomed above him. Anger in her eyes, and just a little sadness. "What is it you once told me, Eric? You didn't believe in chance. Well, you made a convert. I don't believe in chance either. Only making my own opportunities. And I'm making one now. You seduced me to get to my father, and now you're going to pay."

He'd cling to the sadness. Maybe after this was all over he could convince her he really loved her.

Eric couldn't accept the thought that Danni's anger would keep her from him forever.

DANNI SLIPPED OUT of Eric's hotel room and leaned against the door, sucking in huge gulps of air. She'd done it. She'd semi-seduced Eric and left him tied up. So much for being on the straight and narrow.

Without a backward glance, she made a run for it. Her father was going to meet Eric, probably here at the casino. No telling what kind of trap he'd laid out for her dad. She had to cut him off before he arrived.

But where? In the past, before a big con, her father had liked to take a few moments to himself, and get into character. Get into the mark's head. So where

would he go to get into Eric's head. She'd only provided a few sketchy details of her dates with Eric.

The Laundromat? No. Then suddenly she realized where her father would be. It all made sense. She flagged a taxi, giving directions to the Reno arch. Reno prided itself on being the biggest little city in the world. If Daniel Flynn pulled this con off, Reno really would be his gateway to the future.

ERIC COUNTED TO SIXTY before he began working on the weak knot. He didn't need Danni catching him in the act of escaping. He wiggled his left hand, loosening the knot further. Within minutes, he had the rope off and was working on the others.

He should be angry. Getting a guy all primed and ready, then leaving him tied up to be found by housekeeping—not a nice thing to do. But then he had to admire a woman who turned the tables on him.

A shaft of fear spiked through him as he thought of the danger Danni could be putting herself in by trying to save her father. The thugs could be on to her now.

The last knot undone, he shifted off the bed to retrieve his clothes. Thankfully he'd insisted no surveillance cameras in his suite. Even if he brought Daniel Flynn and the rest of the gang to justice, he'd never be able to live down being tied to a bed and left by an asset.

Oh, but Danni was way more than an asset. She was his, and he protected what was his. He raced for his cell phone, pressing the speed dial number for his men.

"Are you tracking her?" he asked without preamble.

"Yeah, she just got into a cab."

"One of ours?" After the hotel's surveillance cameras spotted her getting into a taxi earlier rather than taking her car, Eric had arranged for one to always be available. Complete with geo-positioning trackers and awaiting only one passenger: Danni Flynn.

"I need her exact location now. And a car."

He slapped the cell shut, and slammed it into his pocket. His job had finally begun.

DANNI SPOTTED HER FATHER leaning against a building. The flickering lights from Reno's famous arch reflected off the windshields of nearby cars.

Daniel opened his eyes when he sensed her approach. "Danni-bear, what are you doing here?" A touch of alarm in his voice.

She'd never seen her happy-go-lucky father the least bit concerned. Not even when he'd been sentenced to five years in prison. However, she remembered the one time she'd seen him worried. When he'd come to bail her out of jail.

"I'm trying to stop you."

"Now why would you want to do that?" he asked, smiling, his accent turning European. French. His gaze shifted downward. "It's way too late for that anyway. I'm in too deep."

Danni stared her father in the eyes. "You promised." She spoke quietly, her voice revealing all the pain and disillusionment she'd experienced in the last twenty-four hours.

Her father's face turned serious and he reached for her hand. "I know I did. But just think…this is it. This is my chance. I've finally hit the long con. No more waitress job for you. I'll buy you a house, a car. Whatever you need. Hell, whatever you want. Take care of you the way I could never take care of your mother."

"I don't want any of those things. I'm just like Mom—all I ever wanted was just my dad. And to be normal."

He shook his head. "We're Flynns. We'll never be normal. Why would you even want to be?"

"Yes, we can. Walk away, Dad. That's it. Walk away. We have everything we need. Don't you remember what you've always taught me? Cons are only successful because they exploit the victim's greed. It's only when *we* get greedy…that's when the con goes south."

She squeezed her father's hand. "Let's just go. Get some coffee or something."

Her father took a deep breath and closed his eyes. Relief filled her. *Yes. She'd convinced him.*

When he opened his eyes, his expression turned cheeky. "No can do. You don't even like coffee."

Danni bit back at the frustration. "Then let me tell you, Eric's on to you. He's a fed. I saw his badge."

Instead of her father looking shocked, he simply smiled. "Knew there was something I didn't trust about that boy."

Yeah, Danni remembered Dad's first warning about Eric, teasing her that he was a con man.

"It was a setup all along. He used me to get to you."

"Sorry about that, Danni-bear. Never practiced a romance con myself. No honor in it. You're mad?"

"Hell yes, I'm mad." She'd keep the whole tying up Eric incident to herself.

"Good. Then use that anger to your advantage." He gave her a tight hug. "Join me," he whispered. "We can take that casino for all we need. I'm sure you found plenty of spots we can exploit. Just tell them all to Papa."

As angry as she was at Eric, she wasn't even tempted. Something hard rammed into the middle of her back, propelling her into her father's arms.

"Sounds like a good idea to me," said a cold, angry voice behind her.

"Don't turn around." Her father spoke softly into her ear. With a squeeze to her hands, Daniel Flynn looked over her head to address the person. "Parton. Fancy meeting you here," her father drawled.

"Cut your act, Flynn. I have a gun aimed at your daughter's spine. And you know I don't have a problem with using a gun. Now, this is a touching reunion that I've been looking forward to seeing, but you have my money, Flynn, and I'm ready for you to hand it over."

Her father smiled, only she could see the effort it was taking him to force that grin. "Sure. Let her go, though, you don't need her."

The man behind her jammed the barrel of the gun into her again. She stifled a gasp. *Don't panic.*

"Let her go? But it's taken so long to finally find something you care about, Flynn. So not on your

life. Or hers." The man laughed at his own joke. "She goes nowhere."

Her father patted her on the cheek. "It's okay, Danni. Just a little business," he said, his voice unworried and reassuring.

She looked into his eyes and saw the truth there. *Yeah. They were both going to die.*

Daniel returned his attention to the man with the gun. "Told you before. The money is in Switzerland. You're welcome to join me to get it. You'll have to spot me the cash to retrieve it. Just take that out of my share."

"Ahhh, Flynn, you're funny. Not necessary. Found a banker offshore who'll work the transfer. Let's go."

"Lead the way," her father invited.

"No, you in front, so turn around. I'll give directions." The man her father called Parton pushed the gun into her back to make her walk. Why, oh why, did her father tell her not to turn around so she could see this man? This unknown, hearing only the chill of his voice was way more intimidating.

But then, by not knowing his identity, it could be the one small token that could save her life. Cons were funny like that. Life was funny like that.

Danni worked on swallowing back her fear so she could think.

Keep a clear head. You've been in sticky situations before. Sure, none with a gun at your back, but focus, and do it fast. Once you're off this street, you're dead.

That's when she saw him. Eric. He lurked in the

shadow of a closed storefront, and she almost called out to him. Seeing him untied and dressed and a few feet away from her was almost as satisfying as seeing him naked and tied to the bed.

Oh, more satisfying. Danni could admit that. Just knowing he was nearby made her feel safer. She should focus on being honest.

Calmer now, the irony of the situation hit her. This was just great. Now Eric was in a position to save her. She ground her back teeth together. Danni didn't want him fixing this. She might have to forgive him. She could do her own saving.

What are you, nuts? It was the adrenaline. Adrenaline rushes always made her thinking turn a tad on the tipsy side. If Eric got her out of this situation, she'd thank him without entertaining the notion of kneeing him in the groin. And then she'd leave him again.

Tourists and gamblers milled around them, and she lost sight of Eric. Her would-be kidnapper kept himself and his gun plastered to her back. She felt the panic rise within her again, and her gaze buzzed along wildly until she settled on Eric once more.

Eric pointed to his chest.

What was he trying to tell her? He mouthed something to her as she and her father slowly walked down the sidewalk. Passersby were oblivious to the scenario surrounding them.

Big rack?

It looked as if he was trying to mouth those words. Her mind frantically tried to translate what Eric was

trying to tell her. When had they ever discussed the size of her breasts? Or lack thereof?

Distractions. It hit her. Big racks created distractions. He wanted her to create a distraction. But what kind? Something surprising? Like reaching back and grabbing his package?

Her heartbeat actually kicked up a notch in fear. She swallowed back the inner giggle of hysteria. *Get it together.* The package grab was right out. Too sudden. No quick movements with a gun into her back. She didn't need this slimeball firing the gun into her in shock. Danni's mind raced through a dozen possible scenarios.

She could scream. No, same problem applied.

The begging whimper? Even if her acting skills were up to snuff, she knew in her gut the man behind her had no mercy.

The flop. The oldest hustle in the book. A quick sinking fall to her knees. That's all it would take. If the gun went off, the bullet would maybe hit her shoulder. The only scenario she could imagine. So there'd be no spaghetti straps in her future, at least she'd be alive. She knew it had to be done. Her stomach cramped.

Do it.

Her mind told her to collapse. Her legs weren't ready. Her shoulder kept envisioning the burning, tearing sensation she was sure a bullet would cause.

Eric stood very close to her now, behaving like a guy intent on his cell phone. The man behind her urged her to continue down the busy sidewalk. They were nearing a parking lot. Low lights. Few people.

It had to be now.

Her gaze met Eric's. His brown eyes encouraged her. He believed she could do this. She gave him an almost imperceptible nod, letting him know she was ready.

Then she fell, pushing her father as she went. The rough pavement of the sidewalk cut into her knees.

The man behind her swore, then grunted as a large body swiftly took him to the ground. A shot rang out, and her ears burned from the noise.

Danni braced herself to feel the pain. But nothing came. She turned, wildly searching, only to see Eric grab her attacker's hand and force the gun to clatter to the sidewalk.

She crawled toward it. Soon her fingers wrapped around the hot metal. Parton yelped as Eric's knee jammed into the middle of his back. "You're under arrest," he said, his voice forceful and commanding. And every bit the lawman. Two other men raced toward them. Despite their plain clothing, they smelled like cops.

"Drop the weapon, ma'am," said the stocky one near her. His gun aimed at her head. If she *never* saw or felt another gun pointed in her general direction, it would be too soon.

She gently set the gun on the cement and slid it toward the officer. He tucked it into the back of his waistband, all the while keeping the gun trained on her. "Against the wall."

Where had her silent vow of never being handcuffed again gone? With a sigh, she stood and braced herself

against the rough brick of the building. She positioned her arms and legs in a V. Yeah, she knew the drill.

She glanced over to see her father in much the same stance.

"You did great, Danielle."

She rubbed her face against the scratchiness of the brick, trying to hide the evidence of her tears. The officer grabbed her arm, and "escorted" her to the back of the police car. She scanned the faces around her, but she never saw Eric.

More sirens. Followed by flashing lights, gawkers. The police radio was really hopping so it wouldn't be long before reporters made their appearance. How long she sat there feeling numb and tired and stupid she didn't know, but she knew it was Eric when the passenger's door opened and someone crouched inside to face her.

Somehow it seemed fitting that she'd be across from him in the back seat of a police car.

"You're not under arrest. But you will need to make a statement at the station," he said gently and sounding very, very tired.

She bit her lip to keep from sighing in relief. The man had saved her life, but she was hanging on here to her inner control by a thinning thread. For some reason, not letting this man, who'd used her to get this bust, see any emotion from her felt important.

Danni nodded, and looked outside her window. "I understand."

"Danni, I—"

"Great work, Agent Reed," someone said, slapping him on the back.

So Reynolds wasn't his name. Made sense since she had googled him. Using his real name would have tipped her off. She turned her back from the congratulatory scene playing in front of her eyes. All these officers must know how she'd been duped. Duped into falling in love. Duped into sleeping with Eric. Duped into leading him right to her father.

Now her father would be going to jail. Again, because of her.

A uniformed cop slid behind the wheel of the squad car. "Agent Reed, the Captain has a few questions."

Eric glanced in her direction, his dark eyes probing.

"Not now," she said softly, then tilted her head to look outside the window once more. Not now. Not here. Not ever.

Eric made a noise in the back of his throat as if he wanted to argue with her. But with a nod he left, slamming the car door. She smiled a bitter smile, reveling in the knowledge that if she couldn't make him love her, she could at least make him mad.

And she planned to share every detail of that rope-tying scene in her statement to the police.

15

"I FOUND HIM."

Dirk's three words were like music to Cassie's ears. She gripped the phone tighter, thankful she was between patients. "He's working in a video store at Lake Tahoe. It *is* Kenny. My old roommate."

"Let's go." For canceling, she'd give each patient a free session.

"Cassie, why don't you let me handle this," he told her, his voice laced with caution.

"Not on your life. I want to rip his Internet connection from the wall, then do evil things to him with it a few dozen times. So give me his address."

Cassie made the drive to Lake Tahoe in record time, passing and weaving through traffic that would gain even an Indy driver's respect.

"Damn," she said when she turned on to Kenny's street and found Dirk had already arrived at the home of the man who'd stolen and broadcast some of the most intimate moments of her life. Spite. Greed. She didn't care. This was all about payback, and screw emotional growth. Hell, this would be spiritual growth.

She rammed her car into Park, then nearly sprinted to where the two men were, losing her heels in the process.

Kenny looked pretty good, dazed and sprawled in the middle of his driveway, holding his nose.

"Wow. You hit him," she said, feeling the steam of her anger lessen.

Dirk shook his hand out, his knuckles already turning red. A videotape at his feet. "He had it coming."

"I wanted to be the one to do it," she said.

Dirk angled his head toward Kenny's prone body. "Be my guest."

Instead, Cassie stepped toward her former boyfriend and current lover. Dirk looked amazing. His hair mussed, his muscles tense, he exuded strength and protection. Very Neanderthal. And very, very sexy. She wiped away the touch of blood from Dirk's split lip. "I let him have the first shot."

Then suddenly, she let go of it all. All the anger and hurt she felt toward Dirk. She eyed Kenny as he rolled to his knees, and ran like a coward back into his house.

"Pervert," she shouted.

Dirk stooped to lift the tape from off the ground. "That's that," he said. But he didn't move.

Neither did she. After a moment, she nodded her head toward him. "You know, I think I have a new candidate for chapter nine."

Dirk raised an eyebrow, genuine hope on his face. "Really?" His eyes searched hers. "Just to let you know, my mouth hurts like hell, but a kiss would be worth the agony."

Cassie stood on tiptoe and carefully lifted her lips to Dirk's. This felt so right. So where she should be. Her heart knew it. Her pride still ached.

"I love you, Cassie," he said, his voice harsh with meaning.

Pride be damned. She lowered to her feet and looked up into his eyes. It had been Dirk. Had always been Dirk. "As much as it kills me to say it, I love you, too."

With a groan he hauled her into his arms, wrapping himself around her. "It feels so good to hear that from you. Say it again."

"No," she said against his chest. Smiling, she drew in his woodsy scent.

He chuckled. "I'll never get tired of your sweet mouth. Or your sassy mouth." He handed her the tape. "You know, even though we found this, it doesn't change anything. He could take his images off, but it's been uploaded everywhere."

"For some reason, that tape doesn't bother me as much as it did. My twenty-year-old boobs looked pretty good."

"Your twenty-nine-year-old boobs are outstanding. Although I'd need another look to verify."

She laughed, feeling complete. Feeling light. Feeling loved.

He settled her into her car. After shutting the door, he stuck his head in through the window for one last kiss.

"You know, I knew you'd come around," he said after leaving her breathless.

Cassie waved a finger. "Wait," she said as she fished

a piece of paper from her purse, read it, then slipped it back inside.

"What is that?" he asked, his expression curious.

"Oh, that? I transcribed what you said the other day about how letting me go was your biggest mistake. It's a coping technique I've prescribed in my book. Whenever you irritate me, and I wonder why I'm with you, I pull out that piece of paper and read it."

Dirk cocked an eyebrow. "Really? You feel better and I don't have to do anything else?"

Cassie nodded. "It's the most romantic thing you've ever said to me."

"I thought women went for statements like "I see heaven in your eyes.""

Cassie shook her head. She'd burst out laughing if Dirk ever said those words and meant them. "No. Your telling me you were wrong is far more romantic."

Dirk shook his head, but not seemingly in understanding. He reached for her hands and placed them around his neck, and lightly kissed her lips.

"Cassie," he said, his voice low and seductive. "Whenever you do something that really pisses me off—I'll just think of your ass."

THE LAWYER DANNI HIRED to represent her father picked her up from the police station and dropped her off at her apartment. She wanted a bath, a drink and bed. She always hated the flop. Her knees ached from the scabs she'd gotten when she fell to the sidewalk, but it had probably saved her life tonight.

And Eric.

With the remote, she turned on the TV. She couldn't face the silence of her apartment. She needed noise. Danni unbuttoned her blouse and kicked off her shoes, padding barefoot into her bathroom to turn on the water.

The familiar drumbeats of the evening news filled the air, and she groaned. The news was not what she wanted to hear. She popped back into her front room, only to stop when a picture of Eric Reed, Special Agent in Charge and in action, flashed on her screen.

She was too weary to react.

"Maybe I'll have that drink first."

FIRST IT WAS the ringing of the phone.

Then it was the pounding in her head. Danni lifted her lids.

Wait, that wasn't the phone—it was the door.

She gathered herself together enough to look through the peephole. Her father stood outside.

With a yelp, she tore the door open and flung herself into his arms, her headache chased away by relief.

"Dad, oh, Dad. I was so worried."

Daniel Flynn pulled himself from her arms, and kissed Danni on the cheek. "I hope I never see this look on your face again. Listen, let's go inside. I don't want my 'escort' knowing any more than he has to."

Danni broke from her father's arms, scanning the parking lot in front of her apartment building for any unfamiliar cars. "Don't worry about them," her father said, stepping inside and closing the door behind them.

"Them? As in plural?" When she'd seen her father outside her door, she'd hoped this meant he was a free man.

"I cut a deal," he said, his tone light yet resigned.

She sunk to the couch, guilt pounding her. "This never would have happened if I hadn't gotten involved with Eric."

Her father sat down beside her. "You know how it is. Money and I just don't seem to mix. I still would have gone after it. I still would have gotten caught or killed."

Danni shrugged. "But if Eric—"

"He saved our lives. He told me at the precinct he'd spotted Parton following me for days."

Anger welled up inside her. "But how could my instincts have been so wrong about Eric?"

"Maybe you're more your mother than you are Flynn. In fact, I know you are. Look how easy it's been to make your fresh start. To not go on the grift."

"I'll miss you," she told him in a whisper.

"Come here," he said as he gave her a hug. "I won't be gone as long this time. Full cooperation, and they've already recovered the money."

"How long will you be gone?"

"Nine to thirty-six months. Would have been longer, but Eric leaned on the federal prosecutor to take into account my cooperation and time already served. But no matter how long I'm in, this time when I get out, nothing will be hovering over my head. Maybe I'll even take a page from your book and go straight."

"Really? This isn't a line?"

Her father cupped her face in his hands. "No. I was proud of how you handled yourself last night. I want to make you proud of me."

She blinked back her tears. Flynns didn't show that kind of deep emotion, and she didn't plan to start now.

Later that afternoon, Danni hauled some large cardboard boxes up the stairs to her apartment, the heat of the late afternoon Nevada sun beating down on her neck.

"Let me help you with that."

Danni halted on the stairwell, looking up to see Eric leaning against her front door. Handsome. Sexy. His expression unreadable. Her first inclination was to tell him to back off, she didn't need his help. She didn't need him for anything.

Then she remembered what a lying jerk he was. "By all means, feel free to do all the heavy lifting," she said, shoving the boxes at him.

She entered her apartment and Eric followed her inside. "What are you doing with these?" he asked.

"I'm packing up. I called a court reporting school in Colorado. All my course work will transfer."

He set the boxes down in the kitchen. "Making a fresh start?" he asked.

"Technically, Reno was my fresh start. Except right now the phone won't ring without a reporter asking me about the Vegas heist, my dad or you. I'm not sure if a person is allowed two fresh starts in a lifetime."

Eric winced and looked guilty around the edges. The acting louse. She felt her anger begin to rise.

Which was probably a good thing since she hadn't felt much of anything once her father left her apartment that morning. "Tell me, did you close your eyes when you screwed me?"

"What?" he asked.

Danni stalked into the kitchen, looking for more things to pack.

"Who'd you have to think of in order to make yourself do me? You got a very understanding girlfriend swimming in the pond of scum you emerged from?"

Eric shook his head, his lips set and his chin hard. "There's no one. Only you."

"There is no me. If there was a me, then you'd have to think about how you used me. I'm your mark. You can't confuse the two. I'm not."

He rushed toward her, trying to grab her hands. "Danni, if you'd only listen to me for a minute."

She brushed him off. "What, so I can hear more lies? You must think I am some kind of idiot. Well, why wouldn't you?" she asked, her voice rising. "I certainly gave you no cause to think I use my head. I bet your dad never even tossed around a ball with you."

"What are you talking about?"

"The one personal thing you ever told me, that your dad coached your baseball team, I bet that's not even true. I used to value that memory, fooling myself that you trusted me."

"No, that one is true," he said, trying to get her to meet his gaze.

"That's part of your game, wasn't it? Dole out

tidbits of personal info. I'm a chick. Of course I'd be dying to hear that stuff. Then, when you didn't offer it right away, you knew you had me hooked even more because I was just that much more intrigued. Well, you were right. It worked. I wanted to know everything about you."

Images of their time together flashed across her mind. She felt sick over the treasured memories she was losing. "It's all so clear now. Your technique. Everything you did led me further down the path toward building my trust and to test my resolve. Those security files you 'accidentally' had on your desk. Then left me alone with them in your office. You were betting on me being curious."

"You didn't look."

"Yeah, and you'd know that for sure because you were spying on me. You left me alone in your suite, too. What did you have hidden in there you expected me to find?"

He shrugged, not even looking guilty. "Some fake codes."

"Oh, man. You must have been so bummed when I didn't take the bait. Oh, wait. You just upped the ante. Give the gambler a job in a casino. That's brilliant. What were you hoping for? That I'd mess up and then you could use me as leverage to get my father to cooperate? Now I understand all those subtle questions about him."

"But you never buckled," he said, admiration in his voice.

"That's right. I bet that really ticked you off. Especially after all your hard work." Suddenly she was exhausted. Her shoulders slumped. "Oh, just leave. Why are you even here?"

"I want to explain."

"What's there to explain? You got your man. You even made headlines. Well done, you. I bet you got a promotion, too."

"There is—"

She held up a hand. "I'm not actually interested. I don't want to listen to you. I've listened to you for two weeks now. Everything out of your mouth is a lie."

"Not everything."

"Like I said, I don't want to hear."

"Give me one minute."

"No," she replied, her voice firm. Resolved.

"How about I convince you to listen. We'll play it your way." He pulled a deck of cards from his pocket. "Pick a card. Any card."

She jammed her hands into her pockets. She wasn't picking anything. "What's this about?"

"If I guess your card, then you have to sit down and listen to me for five minutes. That's all I ask. If you still want me to go, I'll go. If I don't guess your card right, I'll admit I was a jerk and be on my way."

"Why don't you just admit you are a jerk and go right now? Besides, you said you only wanted a minute a few moments ago," she reminded him. Actually, if Eric won, which she highly doubted, Danni would use those five minutes to yell at him.

As she had no intention of seeing his lying face again, this would be her only chance. She needed it to be a good one.

He spread the deck out before her. She slipped a card out of the stack, looked at it quickly, knowing her technique didn't allow for any peeking, then stuck it back in the pile.

Eric sifted through the cards for a moment, then pulled one out of the deck and turned the card to face her.

The king of hearts.

Gag. But it was also her card.

"Two out of three," she countered.

"No, I get your five minutes. I'm holding you to the parameters of the bet. Sit."

She reluctantly sat on the couch. Eric crouched down in front of her, cupping her cheeks. "Danni, I did set you up. I work undercover. It's what I do. I never wanted to hurt you. No one does. I just needed to get access to your father."

"Why'd you…why'd you have to do it that way? It's cruel. I treasured those moments with you," she told him, her voice breaking. "Now everything seems so tainted."

Tears? Of course. Now would be the perfect time for her to cry in front of the louse.

He gently wiped away the wetness from her cheeks. "I fell in love with you while making those memories. We'll make new memories together," he said, his voice a promise. "Here. Colorado. My job is flexible."

She rushed to her feet, needing some distance

between them. As she moved, she knocked the cards to the floor. The deck fell to the ground face up.

Every card was a king of hearts.

Her eyes widened as she stooped to pick up a few of the cards. "I can't believe I fell for this old trick. My father—"

"Who do you think taught me that trick?"

She gave him a dubious look. "My dad is a criminal and a thief. I'm not putting a lot of faith in his judgment."

"Your judgment, too. Despite my job and your father, those moments between us were all real."

"I'd believe that a little more if I hadn't spent several hours sitting in an interrogation room last night. I made a promise to myself, too. And despite playing it straight, still found myself locked up."

"All I'm asking for is a chance. You've given your father dozens. Can you give me one?"

"How could I ever believe you enough to give you a chance?" she asked, feeling herself weakening, angry at herself for that weakness. She scrambled to grasp that anger. It sure beat pain and hurt. "You're the first person I've ever trusted outside of my dad and Cassie. You know what we call people who fall for the same con over and over again? A sap."

"You're not a sap."

She nodded. "Not anymore. I could never trust you."

Eric swallowed, his expression grave. "Danni, you were right to trust me. I took that promise I made to you seriously. Let me prove it. You broke into my office. I

know because there's a camera in there. Three, actually."
He grabbed what looked like a CD case from his pocket
and handed it to her.

"What is this?" she asked.

"I made a DVD from the recordings and erased the
originals off the DVR. No one will ever see how adept
you are at B and E. You have the evidence in your hand.
What you do with it is up to you."

Danni gasped.

"I just stole evidence from an investigation and de-
stroyed it. There's the proof. You turn that in, I could lose
my job. Worse. You hold my career, maybe even my
freedom in your hands." He gripped her cold fingers
clutching the DVD case, willing her to believe him. "How
do you feel about me, Danni? Because I love you. I'll
spend the rest of my life proving it if I have to."

She squeezed her eyes tight, feeling some of the heavi-
ness around her heart loosen. "Don't. Don't say that."

"Why not?"

"Because then I have to admit that I love you, too."

He pulled her into his lap. "Would that be bad?" he
asked, tucking her head under his chin.

"Yes," she said. "Very, very bad. It would be so
much easier just to be angry with you. Then you can
never hurt me again."

He held her gently. "I will never give you cause."

Danni took a deep breath and pushed the DVD
toward him. "You better keep it."

"Why?" he asked, looking worried again.

"You decided to trust me. Probably went against

every law enforcement instinct you had for me. I don't ever want this to be between us."

"I love you, Danni."

"Tell me your favorite color."

"Green. Why do you want to know?"

"Because I feel like I don't know you. And I don't make love with people I don't know."

"In that case, I was born in Missouri. I have two younger sisters. No pets. Although I once had a…"

The facts tumbled from Eric Reed, and she smiled.

Sexy. Handy to have around when guns were involved. And not afraid to do a little heavy lifting. She remembered the five dollars she'd hustled from him, and he'd hustled right back on the day they first met.

All in all, he was five dollars well spent.

* * * * *

Happily ever after is just the beginning...

Turn the page for a sneak preview of
A HEARTBEAT AWAY
by
Eleanor Jones

Harlequin Everlasting—Every great love
has a story to tell. ™
A brand-new series from Harlequin Books

Special? A prickle ran down my neck and my heart started to beat in my ears. Was today really special?

"Tuck in," he ordered.

I turned my attention to the feast that he had spread out on the ground. Thick, home-cooked-ham sandwiches, sausage rolls fresh from the oven and a huge variety of mouthwatering scones and pastries. Hunger pangs took over, and I closed my eyes and bit into soft homemade bread.

When we were finally finished, I lay back against the bluebells with a groan, clutching my stomach.

Daniel laughed. "Your eyes are bigger than your stomach," he told me.

I leaned across to deliver a punch to his arm, but he rolled away, and when my fist met fresh air I collapsed in a fit of giggles before relaxing on my back and staring up into the flawless blue sky. We lay like that for quite a while, Daniel and I, side by side in companionable silence, until he stretched out his hand in an arc that encompassed the whole area.

"Don't you think that this is the most beautiful place in the entire world?"

His voice held a passion that echoed my own feelings, and I rose onto my elbow and picked a buttercup to hide the emotion that clogged my throat.

"Roll over onto your back," I urged, prodding him with my forefinger. He obliged with a broad grin, and I reached across to place the yellow flower beneath his chin.

"Now, let us see if you like butter."

When a yellow light shone on the tanned skin below his jaw, I laughed.

"There…you do."

For an instant our eyes met, and I had the strangest sense that I was drowning in those honey-brown depths. The scent of bluebells engulfed me. A roaring filled my ears, and then, unexpectedly, in one smooth movement Daniel rolled me onto my back and plucked a buttercup of his own.

"And do *you* like butter, Lucy McTavish?" he asked. When he placed the flower against my skin, time stood still.

His long lean body was suspended over mine, pinning me against the grass. Daniel…dear, comfortable, familiar Daniel was suddenly bringing out in me the strangest sensations.

"Do you, Lucy McTavish?" he asked again, his voice low and vibrant.

My eyes flickered toward his, the whisper of a sigh escaped my lips and although a strange lethargy had crept into my limbs, I somehow felt as if all my nerve endings were on fire. He felt it, too—I could see it in his

warm brown eyes. And when he lowered his face to mine, it seemed to me the most natural thing in the world.

None of the kisses I had ever experienced could have even begun to prepare me for the feel of Daniel's lips on mine. My entire body floated on a tide of ecstasy that shut out everything but his soft, warm mouth, and I knew that this was what I had been waiting for the whole of my life.

"Oh, Lucy." He pulled away to look into my eyes. "Why haven't we done this before?"

Holding his gaze, I gently touched his cheek, then I curled my fingers through the short thick hair at the base of his skull, overwhelmed by the longing to drown again in the sensations that flooded our bodies. And when his long tanned fingers crept across my tingling skin, I knew I could deny him nothing.

* * * * *

Be sure to look for A HEARTBEAT AWAY,
available February 27, 2007.

And look, too, for
THE DEPTH OF LOVE by Margot Early,
the story of a couple who must learn that love
comes in many guises—and in the end
it's the only thing that counts.

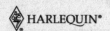

Save $1.⁰⁰ off

the purchase of any Harlequin Everlasting Love novel

Coupon valid from January 1, 2007 until April 30, 2007.

Valid at retail outlets in the U.S. only. Limit one coupon per customer.

5 65373 00076 2   (8100) 0 11302

HEUSCPN0407

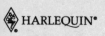

From reader-favorite

MARGARET WAY

Cattle Rancher, Convenient Wife

On sale March 2007.

"Margaret Way delivers…
vividly written, dramatic stories."
—*Romantic Times BOOKreviews*

---

*For more wonderful wedding stories,
watch for Patricia Thayer's new miniseries
starting in April 2007.*

Rocky Mountain
BRIDES

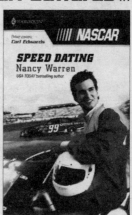

REQUEST YOUR FREE BOOKS!

2 FREE NOVELS PLUS 2 FREE GIFTS!

HARLEQUIN®

Blaze®

Red-hot reads!

HARLE

COMING NEXT MONTH

www.eHarlequin.com

HBCNM0207